W9-BSO-986

Books by Gilbert Rogin

The Fencing Master
What Happens Next?
Preparations for the Ascent

Preparations for the Ascent

PREPARATIONS FOR THE ASCENT

Gilbert Rogin

MIDDLEBURY COLLEGE LIBRARY

RANDOM HOUSE
New York

3/1980
Gen'l

PS
3568
O 48
P7

Copyright © 1979, 1980 by Gilbert Rogin
All rights reserved under International and Pan-American Copyright
Conventions. Published in the United States by Random House, Inc.,
New York, and simultaneously in Canada by Random House of Canada
Limited, Toronto.

Chapter 8 originally appeared in *Harper's*. All the remaining chapters,
excluding chapters 4, 10 and 11, originally appeared in *The New Yorker*
in slightly different form.

Library of Congress Cataloging in Publication Data
Rogin, Gilbert, 1929–
Preparations for the ascent.
I. Title.
PZ4.R734Pr   [PS3568.O48]   813'.54   79-5540
ISBN 0-394-42451-4

Manufactured in the United States of America
98765432
First Edition

To Ring, His Memory

Preparations for the Ascent

ONE

~~~~~~~~~~~~~~~~~

ALBERT TELLS THE STORY of his life—*that* again. Lippholzer richly hums. A composer and arranger, he is being kind enough to score it for Albert—his life, that is.

Lippholzer holds up a hand, as though shushing the brass. "Not exactly what one would call Brahmsian," he murmurs.

Albert tells him that he never represented his life as such, that cinematically speaking, which, after all, is how we're looking at it, he sees it as one that might befall a fat Montgomery Clift.

Lippholzer makes a face and unfolds his napkin. They are in a French restaurant, about to have lunch.

The reason Albert brought in Lippholzer is that for some time he's felt there's been something missing in his life. Music is what suddenly came to him, swelling, as in a movie.

He had called Lippholzer up to tell him about it.

"Please?" Lippholzer had said.

"I was watching this commercial," Albert had said. "Two young marrieds. In Miami Beach. By moonlight. They're swimming to a sixty-five-piece symphony orchestra."

"So?" Lippholzer had said.

"So when my wife and I are in Miami all I hear is sixty-five air-conditioners, every one of them on 'hi cool.'"

"I could get the London Philharmonia," Lippholzer is saying, bending his noble head to his Bloody Mary. "But for you it would be a waste. From what you're telling me, your life, it is strictly low-budget."

Albert tells him it never crossed his mind it couldn't be brought in for under a million.

"I am going to put together for you," Lippholzer says, "a woodwind quintet—a little piccolo for your comical childhood—supplemented by three trombones—so solid, your college education—two percussion, harp, four celli—how sad! how jubilant!—a bass, a guitar. These will amply take care of any moment in your life. I underscore the oboe in your case. What a pathetic instrument! When you are alone, I do the whole thing on the oboe."

Albert tells him there's going to be an awful lot of oboe.

"Do me a favor," Lippholzer says. "You do the living and leave the music to me."

A FEW days later, following Lippholzer's advice, Albert is on his way to the twenty-fifth reunion of his high-school class. This is to take place in the dining hall where once they lunched on tuna-fish casserole and macaroni and cheese. Albert has ridden the subway to the end of the line and is toiling dismally up the hill. The ruin I will note in my classmates will tacitly be noted in me, he muses, so I will age twenty-five years in a few minutes.

It is late May, early evening, and the trees beneath which Albert passes are in full leaf. He lifts his eyes and is made dizzy, as though he were being crushed to their massive and odorous bosoms. Not my kind of simile, granted, he thinks—but do I hear music in the air already?

Albert takes the shortcut through the patch of woods. There it is nearly dark, wilder, and his way more steep: shades of Dante, he acknowledges. He gets a whiff of the past, an emanation, he supposes, in which verdure, rot, damp, mold, earth, pollen, car exhaust, and dog do are commingled, and for an instant he is able to visualize a boy (a character, however, so nearly imaginary that the fact that he bears Albert's name and resembles him seems an astonishing coincidence) traipsing up the hill with a brief-case. What books does it hold, Albert wonders. *Silas Marner? Ethan Frome*, P-40s and Zeros, guns blazing, on the end papers? What expectations is he carrying about in his head?

Albert reflects: Through the years, any number of people have played the role that has become known as my life: I would but faintly recognize them, their lines, businesses. As I have often remarked, I seem to vanish behind me like footprints on a mud flat. Of course, I do not deny the possibility that my life has a hidden con-tinuity. Oedipus comes to mind. But suppose he knew what he was up to all along. Or suppose he *once* knew but forgot. Or, even, that he was indifferent. These versions would be as tragic as the traditional one, perhaps more so.

A reunion I would more gladly go to would be one of my earlier selves, Albert reflects. He pauses on a footbridge in the woods to consider that somber assembly. (Earlier in the spring, the melting snow would have formed a torrent below him, a touch Albert associates with Boswell preparing himself for his great interview with Rousseau by pensively strolling along a similar stream, the romantic prospect giving his thoughts "a vigorous and solemn tone." Now, however, the streambed is dry and littered with trash.)

To keep my reunion manageable, Albert thinks, I'd invite who I was at each quarter of each year in my life, so that if everybody showed we'd have a crowd of a hundred and sixty or so. I can see us all, in some Crystal or Palm Room, the oldest with the youngest in their arms. This is apposite, for, being childless, I have been my own child. An accordionist is playing standards. Looking appealingly into our nearly forgotten faces, we wonder what has happened and what lies ahead.

"You call this living?"

Not Vergil, nor Laius, nor Mlle. Le Vasseur, coming to conduct Albert to the Savage Philosopher, but a postman, going downhill with an empty bag. No, not even he. It is Lippholzer, who joins Albert on the bridge. They gaze at the refuse together.

Albert asks him how come he's all dressed up like that.

"I'm doing research," he says.

Albert asks him what a scene like this inspires him to compose.

"*Bupkis*," he says. "For nothing scenes I write nothing. Let me clue you in, it would wind up on the cutting-room floor."

AT THE reunion, Albert is cornered by Roger Russek. They drink sherry out of plastic cups. Except for his hair, which is entirely gray, Russek looks exactly as Albert remembers him—more precisely, as he looked when they were fellow-scientists in their senior play, *R. U. R.*, and they powdered one another's hair. Albert has the feeling that Russek never grew up, or that he is a well-coached impostor. His insistence on dredging up lurid episodes from their school days reinforces the latter impression.

"You remember Norman Greenberg?" Russek says.

"No," Albert says.

"He was with us in fifth grade," he says.

"Were you in fifth grade with me?" Albert says.

"You remember when Norman's science experiment exploded?"

"No."

"We took him to the nurse's office, you and I."

"I don't remember."

"You were leading him along and I was bringing up the rear, wiping the blood off the floor with paper towels."

"I don't remember."

"He kept saying, 'I'm blind. I'm blind.'"

"I remember," Albert says. But, he reflects, I thought it was myself, when *my* experiment exploded.

"Greetings, gates. Give me five."

Lippholzer is before them, hand outstretched. Like them, he is wearing a name tag. His reads, "Dr. Lippholzer, Music."

"How are you, Dr. Lippholzer?" Russek asks.

"Crazy. Another year, another 'Hallelujah Chorus.' I could have used you cats. My basses were nowhere."

Russek goes for a refill. Lippholzer laughs like a rhinoceros, like Dr. Johnson. "Campus character," he explains. "By the way, I couldn't help but overhearing your conversation with that person. For that I would dash off a divertimento in F minor for the bassoon and piccolo, with a soupçon of French horn thrown in for poignancy."

Russek gives Albert a lift home so he won't have to take the subway. As they drive down the Henry Hudson Parkway, Russek says, "There is no integrity anymore." Albert merely nods in agreement. It is night and Albert is smelling the incoming tide. Farther on, Russek says that he took his son up the Amazon last winter. "I always liked science," he adds. Albert pictures the Russeks, father and son, at evening, aboard a river steamer, contemplating the great, dark flood astern, the darker banks. Russek takes a snapshot from his inside jacket pocket and shows it to Albert. It is of the scene Albert imagined.

They stop at a toll booth on the bridge spanning Spuyten Duyvil. As Russek fumbles for change, the toll collector winks at Albert. Lippholzer.

"Strings in a low register!" he shouts as they drive off. "Harp and Latin percussion lightly in the background!" He bursts into song: "La-dah-dah-dah-*dum*-la-dee-dee-dah-dah-dah-*dum*."

Russek pulls up at the door of the restaurant where Albert is meeting his wife, Violet. Albert prevails upon him to join them. He can only stay a minute, he says, as he is getting up early to ride in the Park. Albert sets him there, amid fanciful mists, posting. This elegant pose cannot be sustained. If there is an illiberality among us Jews, Albert tells Russek, it is because we never learned to sit a horse; we missed out on the whole cavalry *schmear*. While everyone who was anyone in Western Europe was on horseback, absorbing grace, bearing, panache through the seat of his pants, the Jew was *schlepping* on foot. In the nineteenth century, when he finally arrived, it was by carriage.

"I never cared for history," Russek says.

They enter the restaurant. Violet is seated at the bar, bent over the *Times* crossword puzzle. Albert introduces her to Russek.

"Roger and I went to school together," Albert explains.

"Do you remember how we used to look down the front of Señora Ramírez y Ramírez' dress when she went over our *exámenes*?" Russek says.

"Did we see anything?" Albert says.

"Which way is the little boys' room?" Russek says.

Albert looks over Violet's shoulder at the upper left-hand corner of her puzzle:

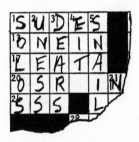

"What's this 'sudes' you've got for 'Secular people'?" he says. "Marketplace of old is 'leata'? 'Uness' is a 'Scottish county'?"

"I didn't know them," she says, "so I made them up."

Russek is passing among the tables, handing out snapshots, like tracts, of what he and his son saw from the stern.

Albert reflects: So often illusions cannot support the symbolic weight they are meant to carry; Russek's dimly perceived river falls into this category, as do my wife's definitions. The team of horses awaiting me in the woods is yet another example. Tonight I will dream that I was to drive them into Yankee Stadium for a Giants game. These absurd notes always intrude. I will be led to believe that the team—are there two horses or four?—has been tethered in a clearing, but I won't know where and I will have mislaid the reins. I will have the feeling that more time has elapsed than I have accounted for, that I was supposed to have gone after them days ago, and that by now they have dropped in their traces. In the poor, brown light with which I am going to grace the scene, the fallen horses look like a pile of old rugs. None of this will be found in anything I tell Lippholzer or will ever be orchestrated. (Nor, as in Bach—I'm thinking of "Vor deinen Thron tret' ich hiermit," composed on his deathbed—will the numerical equivalent of my name be resplendently revealed, the quavers correspond to the beat of the human pulse.)

One order of wonders might be: things seen; things unseen; things seen in dreams; things unseen in dreams.

Also, I must resist the temptations of pessimism.

A porter comes out of the kitchen with a bucket of ice. He hands it to the bartender, who empties it into a sink. The sound is of, simultaneously, a roll on a cymbal and a roll on a timpani shell. The porter turns and points to a corner table. Lippholzer again. Albert follows his finger with his eyes. A man is seated at the table, wearing a well-worn dinner jacket. On Lippholzer's cue he raises an oboe to his lips.

TWO

ALBERT SAYS, "I was swimming with my eyes closed. Breaststroking. But before long I realized that I wasn't getting anywhere, that what I was swimming in no longer had the consistency of water."

Violet says, "What would you say it had the consistency of?"

"Let's say it had a granular consistency. I opened my eyes and I was lying on my stomach on a sidewalk on the Upper East Side, ineffectually breaststroking in several inches of snow. Some children were watching."

"It sounds to me like a dream of old age."

SHAVING, naked, still wet from the shower, Albert sees in the medicine-chest mirror a person standing behind him, shrouded in steam. He holds up what seems to Albert to be a cloak, and makes to wrap him in it. Albert thinks: My time has surely come. Instead, the person starts drying Albert's back. It is Barney, his stepson, aged seventeen. "Blot, don't rub," Albert says.

"You shave too recklessly," Barney says, patting Albert here and there with the towel.

Albert slows down. Barney raises Albert's left arm, which, Albert surmises, must have been hanging by his side, dries beneath it, guides it back into place.

"If I fell in battle," Barney says in Albert's tone of voice, "he would thus tenderly arrange my limbs."

He is putting me on, Albert reflects, but the sentiment is affecting, and his choice of words and imagery shows wider reading than I had suspected.

ALBERT flies to Miami, speculating on futurity. Upon his return, he tells Violet of an exceptional incident. He had arrived late at night, changed into a bathing suit, put on his little plastic goggles to protect his eyes from the chlorine, and gone to the motel pool, which was illuminated by two underwater lights at the deep end. A Cuban boy of ten or twelve was in the shallow end. Although it was Albert's impression that the boy was climbing out of the pool while he was diving in, as Albert approached the wall to make his turn he saw the boy's dark, slender, headless body before him.

Violet says at this point, mimicking Albert, "There's no one else in the whole pool except me and him, so, of course, he has to do a number in my lane."

"It's not fair," Albert says.

"At the Y, the guy in front of me always gets a towel with more nap on it than I do," Violet says.

"The guy behind me gets one with more nap, too," Albert says. "Didn't he see me coming? Wasn't he going to get out of the way? His figure loomed larger."

"I was going to have to smack him one," Violet says.

"I was going to have to brush him aside," Albert says. "Instead of dropping my hand slightly below the diagonal at the point of entry, I rotated it outward—"

"So I could give him a brush in the mouth," Violet says.

"What I was going to do," Albert says, "was make contact, touch, and execute my turn all in one fluid motion. But as I extended my hand he held out his to mine."

"Like God giving life to Adam," Violet says.

"Along those lines," Albert says. "My fingers touched the tiles and I was joined to my writhing shadow."

The above discourse has taken place in bed. Dwelling on his unresisting drift, Albert prepares to rise.

As my readers—they are Albert's too, it seems superfluous to note—Violet, and Josh, Albert and Violet's dachshund, are well aware, Albert frequently gets up in the middle of the night. My readers know because I have touched on it in previous works. Violet knows because Albert wakes her up and tells her. "I've got to go to the bathroom," he may say. (If he's not sure she heard him, he enlightens her on the return trip; e.g., "I had to go to the bathroom.") Or "I think I'll get something to eat." (Sometimes he expatiates. For example, "I'm torn between a sardine sandwich on health bread and a bowl of Granola." A corollary to this might be, reawakening her: "Nobody told me there aren't any sardines.") Or, simply, "I can't sleep." (The corollary to this, as to so much, is "It's not fair.") Josh's knowledge is presumed. Although Josh gives few signs of it, it is Albert's belief that he knows what's

· 13 ·

going on—not understands, *knows*. What else could account for his jumping into Albert's lap the other night and pleading with him to unburden his heart.

Who knows Albert best? Let's find out. "Are you sleeping?" "Yes," Violet says. "But who knows me best?" "Your readers know as much of you as you've ever acknowledged," she says. "I know as much of you as you've ever acknowledged and almost everything else. Josh knows nothing that you've acknowledged, but he knows everything else."

With that, Albert puts on his slippers and sets out for the kitchen. En route, he passes Josh, curled up on the living-room couch. Josh opens an eye—keeping tabs on me, Albert acknowledges. The kitchen light is on, and Emily, Albert's stepdaughter, is bent over the stove, stirring the contents of a saucepan with a wooden spoon. She is nineteen and lives with Sean, who's into yo-yos, in the Intergalactic College of Love. This, she has explained, is neither a crash pad nor a commune but "a whole bunch of people doing a trip separately but in the same house." From time to time she comes home to see what's in the refrigerator or if there are any new magazines, and to look at herself in the full-length mirror.

"You're cooking something at 2 A.M.?" Albert says.

"No," she says, without averting her head.

Albert approaches and looks over her shoulder. Agitated by boiling water so that it appears alive, obscured by bubbles, is something blue and white, evidently flowered.

"Then what are you doing?"

"Shrinking my underpants."

Albert reserves comment.

"Many years ago, I went with a nurse," she says, imitating Albert. "Once, when I had occasion to use her bathroom, the tub was full, and in it giant, pale jellyfish almost imperceptibly writhed. As it turned out, she was soaking her uniforms."

"I've boiled my eggs in that pan for fourteen years," Albert tells Violet when he returns to bed. She is lying on her side, facing the wall. He cups her head with his hand. Sometimes, when she is too weary or too deep in sleep to reply, she communicates by shaking her head. Now, however, the movement is so slight—the least tremor—that he is unable to tell whether she is sympathetic (up and down) or, once more, fed up to here (side to side).

It is at this point that Albert hears someone playing the piano. I must explain that Albert and Violet live on the third floor, in the rear, and that their windows look out on what amounts to an immense airshaft; that is, although there are several neglected gardens below, strewn with sooty, rain-soaked toys, they are walled in by the backs of two other apartment houses and two loft buildings, one occupied by a machine shop, the other seemingly empty save for an acting studio.

From their windows you have to crane your neck to see the sky, and Albert has never observed a woman disrobing or a migratory bird. In the day there is the whine of machinery, at night unearthly cries. When Albert and Violet moved in, they thought these were the product of passion or violence, but they soon learned that the cries came from the acting studio.

Albert called the police.

"Sixth Precinct. O'Hanrahan speaking."

"Officer O'Hanrahan, people are screaming outside my window."

"Yes."

"You can't hear them?"

"No."

"If you'll hang on a minute, I'll stick the receiver outside the window."

"That won't be necessary."

"It won't take a second. I've got a long cord. Did you hear *that*? Are you still *there*?"

"We can't do anything about it until after eleven. If it's still going on then—"

"They're actors and actresses."

"—I'll send a couple of men over."

To return to the piano music. In the drab, barbarous setting I've described, its notes glitter like a toad's eye. Albert gets up and peers through the blinds. One window is lit. Albert sees a man in pajamas playing Mozart's "Fantasy in C Minor." Actually, all Albert can see of him is his left hand, a pajama sleeve. In the cadenza, more of him comes into view: for instance, his unshaven cheek, his right hand. The sixty-fourths defeat him. He falls behind, breaks off, starts the cadenza anew. Again he cannot keep the tempo. He strikes wrong notes, stops. He will never reach the andantino. His left hand holds a chord, but it has died out or is so faint Albert can no longer hear it. Albert imagines the man's right hand supporting his head— a pose Albert is acquainted with.

The man arises and approaches the window, and Albert sees that he is him, too—that is, in the sense that he could be Albert's shadow cast across the dismal gulf. The impression is so vivid that Albert hesitates to move lest it be confirmed.

"How to account for this melancholy apprehension,"

Violet says in further imitation of Albert. "I never got beyond 'Little Keyboard Frolics.'"

"I did."

"How far?"

"'More Little Keyboard Frolics.'"

A DAY or two later Albert gets out of bed under the scrutiny of cats. One cat is looking him over from the floor, another is looking him in the eye from a radiator cover, a third is looking down at him from the top of a bookcase, its tail swishing in front of a set of Carlyle. (It has often been Albert's lot to be thrown in among cats. No good has ever come of it.) On this occasion, the bed is not his own, and it is 1:30 P.M.

"Have they been there the whole time?" Albert says to the person still in bed, who nods. "Did they see everything?" She nods again. "Do you think they'll remember what they saw?"

"If they do," she says, "they wouldn't dream of telling my husband."

Albert thoughtfully puts on his socks.

"What are you doing?"

"I'm going."

"But you've only been here forty-five minutes."

"I've got to go to the Y."

"Go later."

"Then I'll have to swim in the small pool. They kick you out of the large pool at two-thirty. Actually, I have to be in the water by two-ten, because it takes me twenty minutes to do my laps. My record is fifteen minutes and fifteen seconds. I was younger. Also, I may have miscounted."

"Oh."

"The large pool is twenty-five yards long, the small pool is twenty, so if I start out in the large pool and am obliged to switch to the small pool, I have to do this math in my head while I'm swimming, to figure out how many small-pool laps I have to swim in addition to the large-pool laps I've already swum to make them add up to a half mile—which is how far I swim—and I lose track of what number lap I'm swimming."

"What do you do in that case?"

"I go back to the last recollected lap."

"So don't go until later and do all your laps in the small pool."

"You make more turns in the small pool than you would swimming the same distance in the large pool. There's more pushing off. When you push off you're not swimming, you're gliding. In other words, to swim the equivalent of a half mile in the large pool you have to swim . . . Besides, the water's warmer. They always keep the water in the small pool warmer than the water in the large pool, and the water in the large pool is too warm."

"Why don't you ask them to lower the temperature?"

"I do. They tell me the older members complain when the temperature is below eighty. I tell them it's the *Young* Men's Christian Association. They tell me they can't disregard a member's feelings just because he has grown old. 'Ah, you will grow old, too,' they tell me."

"Why don't you skip the Y altogether for a day?"

"But then I couldn't weigh myself."

"Run that by me again."

"I weigh myself every day I go swimming. There's a scale at the Y."

"What would happen if you didn't weigh yourself one day?"

"It would leave a gap."

"A gap?"

"Or lacuna. Each day, I put my weight down in an appointment book. I've got books going back nine or ten years. You can spot trends."

"For one day, couldn't you put a weight down without actually weighing yourself? You could approximate it."

"I wouldn't dream of falsifying my weight."

"It wouldn't be a falsehood if you never actually *weighed* yourself."

"If I didn't weigh myself, I wouldn't put my weight down. It's an historical document. It reminds me of who I am."

By this time, Albert is knotting his tie. He is at the window, looking out.

"Do you see that apartment over there," she says, joining him. "The other night we heard someone playing the piano. We couldn't see him. The piano is out of sight."

"It might have been a recording."

"He kept making mistakes and starting all over again."

Albert muses: If my life were of my devising, through the windows of the apartment she indicated I would see the marble-topped table at which I write. Josh would be curled before my open dictionary, having leaped on the chair on which I sit while I write, and from there gained the table, as though he had sought to look up something I had not satisfactorily defined and, finding the task beyond him, given himself over to sleep. I would mark how he resembled the marble dogs that lie at the marble feet of effigies—often, in fact, support them. And I would recall that when I went to the yard to buy the stone for my table-top the man dashed a pail of water on the great, un-polished slab, revealing its color and pattern.

"But the moment passes," she says, evidently imper-sonating Albert.

As ALBERT goes down her stairs on the way to the Y, he is made aware, as he was when he climbed them, of a pervasive, musty odor. It is, Albert realizes, a smell he associates with the stairwells of poorly maintained brown-stones, which, in the years before his marriage, he would ascend to see one girl or another who dished up casseroles and put Vivaldi on the phonograph while making love.

Once again it is borne in upon Albert that his life is repeating itself, only this time around he has to pause on the landings on the way up to catch his breath, and WCBS-FM has superseded "The Four Seasons." In another ten years, he thinks, I will have reached the point I am at now —between the third and second floors, on the way down— and so forth.

A man climbing up draws abreast of Albert. He is wear-ing modified bells and has luxuriant gray sideburns—pos-sibly the husband. As their paths cross, the man murmurs, "My life stands revealed as a Sisyphean ordeal, with Groucho Marx as Sisyphus, a partly deflated beach ball for a boulder." The conceit isn't half bad, Albert admits, but the imitation is barely acceptable.

It would behoove me to change, Albert concludes, to see another class of girl—a stewardess, say, or cocktail waitress, with a Dynel pouf and a twenty-four-hour door-man, a girl who reads Jeane Dixon and says "shirr" for "sure."

"May I . . . ?"

"Shirr."

"Do you like it when I do this?"

"Shirr."

"And this?"

"Shirr."

"How about me? Do you like me a little bit?"

"Shirr."

"Do you agree with Kierkegaard when he says, 'It is perfectly true, as philosophers say, that life must be understood backwards. But they forget the other proposition, that it must be lived forwards. And if one thinks over that proposition it becomes more and more evident that life can never really be understood in time, simply because at no particular moment can I find the necessary resting place from which to understand it—backwards'?"

"Shirr."

"I JUST called to let you know that I didn't weigh myself."

"You *didn't?*"

"There wasn't any scale. Evidently, it was inaccurate, for it was taken out to be repaired."

"I see."

"I'm up in the air."

ALBERT goes to one of Barney's basketball games. Barney has forbidden Albert to speak to him at half time or after the game; he is also not allowed to speak to the coach or even to the official scorer to see how many points Barney got. For this, and for other desolating reasons, Albert gets on the officials. You may have heard him: "On the arm! *On the arm!*"

Barney is taken out in the second quarter and never

reappears—doesn't "get any more light," as he would say. From his seat high in the crowded bleachers, Albert gazes down at him on the bench across the court, impassive, resplendent in his shimmering purple-and-gold uniform, and shakes his head. By this he means to reassure Barney of the strength of his affection—that he doesn't know why the coach doesn't put him back in, either, and that his, Albert's, life is tremendously sad. Barney doesn't respond.

That evening when Barney comes home, Albert asks whether he saw him at the game.

"I always see you," he says.

"Did you see me shaking my head?"

"You always do that."

ALBERT'S mom calls. "As you know," she says, "I've been lying here sick, so I've had the opportunity to think about that old pile-lined coat you insist on wearing. It's unworthy of a man in your position."

"Don't give it another thought, Ma."

"But it's falling apart. It makes you look like one of those derelicts you see. Even Sean wouldn't wear something like that. You've exhausted it. Ragged pieces flap about."

"The coat has assumed too much prominence in your life, Ma."

"No, in yours. You even chose to wear it when you came to lunch with me and Dad, and we live in a conventional neighborhood. Abercrombie's having a sale on pile-lined coats. Dad's willing to forgo his lunch hour and meet you there."

"I'm forty-two years old."

"And you've been wearing that coat since you were sixteen. Are you trying to set a record at my expense?"

* * *

VIOLET says, "Guess what happened to me today?"

Albert says, "I give up."

"I went to Dr. Prigozy for a checkup, and he said I had grown more than an inch. Last year I was five one and a quarter. Now I'm five two and a half."

"Forty-three-year-old people don't grow."

"Won't you let something exceptional happen to me?"

"I'm calling Prigozy."

While Albert dials, the immense suburban hedges against which so many nineteenth-century ideologues, autodidacts, crackpots posed for their photographs come to mind—great, rank barriers imaginably stories high, through whose dense and mysterious foliage tram bells, footfalls but faintly penetrated.

"I hope I'm not disturbing you, Dr. Prigozy, but are you really of the opinion that it is possible to grow when you're past forty?"

ALBERT enters the Intergalactic College of Love. Emily and Sean live in the basement. This is his first visit. He sits on a mattress on the floor, alongside Emily, and they hold a conversation. It lasts nearly an hour—by far the longest they've ever had. As they speak, it grows dark. Sean is practicing with his electric yo-yo. He does a man-on-the-flying-trapeze. He rocks the baby. He does a double-brain-twister. He does a sleeping-beauty. He walks the dog. He does an around-the-world. The fiery yo-yo swings about the darkened room like a heavenly body.

Albert struggles to his feet. "I've got to go," he says.

Emily accompanies him upstairs. In the foyer, they come to a stop before a hand-lettered notice: "Vacuum Bee, 11 P.M."

"I wonder what *that* is," she says, giggling.

Albert thinks: She could be six—an age at which I didn't know her, she me. If we had, we might have rescued each other. I want to hug her. There is no precedent. I write this in longhand, consoled by my familiar loops, my bars, my terminal strokes. These are my lineaments.

THREE

~~~~~~~~~~~~~~~~~~

PEOPLE LEAD THEIR LIVES DIFFERENTLY. You can't crouch in hides, watch them like grebes or gibbons, and draw specific conclusions. Consider, if you will, Albert requests, that man who bears such a heartbreaking resemblance to myself, weeping into his dinner tray at thirty-three thousand feet. Heading south at an airspeed of five hundred and twenty miles an hour, what grief has overtaken him? Just this: He put salt and pepper on his mashed potatoes. Then, taking up his fork, he made to plunge it into the plastic dish. Grains of salt and pepper flew every which way, including that of his impending face. He had struck a sheet of Saran Wrap protecting the potatoes, which he had not noticed. He laid down his fork, removed the Saran Wrap, and salted and peppered the potatoes anew. Picking up the fork again, he took his first bite. The mashed potatoes was banana pudding. This could not happen to everyone. Offhand, Albert would say it would occur once every five hundred thousand passenger-miles. The emotional reaction is less unusual. Feelings are accentuated at altitude, even in a pressurized cabin.

But who can say what will undo one? For instance, here is the same exceptional fellow sitting by himself late at night in the Sans Souci Launderama, in a Miami shopping center, shedding tears at sea level. Except for the Sans Souci, in which fluorescent tubes distribute their forbidding light on the ranks of washers and dryers, the notices advertising babysitters, lost cats, and used potter's wheels, the shopping center is dark. What's the matter? First off, the decline of Arabic numerals. He had glanced at his watch to see when his wash would be done. Although the watch wasn't new, only then did he realize there were no numbers on its face. In their place was a series of inconsequential dashes. It must have been years since he had seen numerals on a watch face. He envisioned the missing figures, was moved by the elegance of their lines, and arrived at the opinion that man had never designed anything finer, "3" and "5" having pride of place, although, he acknowledged, there might be those who would plump for "2." The several alphabets suffered by comparison, as did mathematical symbols, toasters, cathedrals. Against these he arrayed great works of nature—striped bass, roses, shearwaters, disrobed women. He pictured a vast plain upon which the pick of both classes of things was forming up, as though to pass in review, and was struck by how much he took for granted and, equally, by how much he had failed to take seriously. If you had these or similar imaginings in the middle of a rinse cycle, would you, too, be brought to grief?

Under certain circumstances, playing footsie can have much the same effect. For this demonstration, put yourself in the shoes of our hero. More literally, put yourself in his socks. Behold him, one of a party of six, sitting at a small round table in the cocktail lounge of a Holiday Inn, playing footsie with a stewardess whose name is either Lauri, Audri, or Kelli. He has slipped off his right loafer—on the principle, he supposes, that if he is right-handed he is bound to be right-footed, and he wants to give it his best shot—and is caressing one of her feet with his instep. At the same time, he is watching her face for her reaction. Nothing. He has grown old. He has lost his touch. He knocks a book of matches off the table—a ruse—and stoops to retrieve it. Beneath the table everything is murky, dismal, and tangled, like a mangrove swamp. To sort things out, he takes hold of his right leg at the knee and gropes downward toward his unproductive foot. He has been playing footsie with his own cast-off loafer. As Rousseau said, my pen falls from my hand.

ALBERT thinks: My dad is as sensible as the next man, but none of the above could happen to him, so it would be idle even to speculate on his responses. He doesn't own a pair of loafers. He disapproves of loafers. He considers my wearing them perverse. "Loafers don't offer enough support," he says. ("Your feet flop around in them," Albert's mom chimes in. "We brought you up to respect your feet.") When Albert's dad goes on a trip, he takes drip-dry garments, which he washes in the sink before retiring. "A moment's application," he says pointedly. Albert's dad thinks that Albert is apathetic. Albert submits that what he is, in fact, is immobilized, the Apollonian and Dionysian sides of his character being of equal strength. Albert's dad also considers it an affront to season your food before tasting it.

Although Albert's dad keeps his guard higher than Albert does his, blows do get through, as the next episode so poignantly illustrates.

Albert would have thought he had visited his dad's office only a couple of months ago, but more time must have gone by, he realizes, for how much has changed. Not in his office *per se*—that is immutable—but in the long, straight, insufficiently lit corridor that leads to it. (Albert calls it "insufficiently lit" out of deference to his dad. He once referred to it as "dismal," to which his dad took exception. He said Albert tended to be eisegetical, that the corridor was merely insufficiently lit. They don't always see eye to eye, Albert and his dad.) What's different is that the names on the doors along the way are new. In the past, they were Jewish. On occasion, Albert would come across their bearers in the men's room, absorbed in combing their hair with both hands. Operators, Albert's dad called them. Now the frosted-glass doors read: Taiwan Consolidated Corp.; Interglobal Philippine Import, Ltd.; Mitsobushi American, Inc.

"You're being overrun," Albert tells his dad.

"My secretary tells me their girls make rice in the ladies' room," his dad says in what Albert would definitely call a dismal tone of voice.

How would you like to be seventy-five and hear the rumble of furniture-laden dollies drawing near?

How would you like to be forty-three, Albert asks, and hear, first thing in the morning, a dachshund awakening, shaking himself? The sound is like that of slatting sails, and proposes imponderable voyages, whales' grandiose sighing. For an instant, another version of life seems possible. Then the blower in the machine shop next door is switched on, as it is every weekday at eight. It roars yet as I write, Albert would like to let you know. What recourse does Albert have? He could seek out the shop manager and fall on his knees. He could encourage Josh to go on the standpipe by the shop door. After the roar, a resounding crash—Barney letting his weights down in his bedroom. Before going to school he presses his body weight (one hundred and fifty pounds)—three sets of five reps. He is developing his shoulders and arm extensors so he can beat me up, Albert realizes. Following the crash, a whine. The volume increases as Albert approaches the living room. Sean is standing naked before the full-length mirror, dreamily wielding the power detangler Violet bought him for his twenty-fifth birthday.

Albert goes through the mail. It includes a rejection slip from a French publisher. ". . . *Avec nos regrets, veuillez agréer l'expression de nos sentiments les meilleurs.*" Albert realizes he is not fully conversant with *agréer*. He is about to get down the French-English, English-French dictionary when he recalls that Emily tore out nearly all the French-English "A"s and a good many of the "B"s several years ago. He cannot remember what he did to annoy her or why her revenge took the form it did, but he can still hear the terrible ripping.

As you may have noted, so far not a word has been spoken in Albert's household. The following occurs to him: If you've been confined to bed for a long time, your first steps would be weak, hesitant. The same could be said in connection with other parts of the body. Not the tongue. Albert has gone for days without speaking to anyone but waitresses and cabaña boys. When he did he was as eloquent as ever, perhaps more so. Albert is sure he is not alone in this regard. He submits that if he didn't utter a word for a year, his first cogent, mellifluous sentences would make men sit up and take notice, cry, laugh, whichever his intent. Given a year to get it right, he is convinced he could sweet-talk the thrush from his thicket, have him singing to him from his wrist. So it is with the general plan of my life, Albert recognizes, but although I have been tinkering with it all these years, it may not be workable. The possibility exists that instead of seeking solace in assonances I should be stilling the discord in the faithless arms of Lauri, Audri, or Kelli.

Albert supposes he was attempting something of that sort when he haunted the Sans Souci Launderama late at night, helping divorcées and widows fold their laundry and reciting snatches of Gerard Manley Hopkins to them above the hum, whir, whine, and clank of Big Boys. A divorcée who shall be called C—— dates from that romantic period. If it can be said that we have ruling principles, hers was carnality; Albert's is less easily expressed. What he supposes he's doing is trying to pick every last shred of flesh from his life so that he may contemplate the serene, gleaming bone. Bear in mind—Albert does—that in the end this may have a different, less consoling shape than he had anticipated.

When Albert made love to C——, he gazed down at her broad, slightly domed forehead. Almost no flesh was interposed between the skin and the frontal bone. As she struggled to be once more free of the weight of her life, what little light there was slid across the curve of her forehead, making it appear harder, bleaker, nearly phosphorescent; the illusion was that as a consequence of her exertions the skin split, revealing the bone.

Albert recalls thinking at the time that they could not be

less alike but that they are heading in the same direction, she convulsively, eyes shut, he painstakingly, looking where he's going, and that at this point she is out front, and that these are the chances you take.

Nowadays Dr. Nathan Nederlander is the pilot of Albert's soul. "I'm turning the wheel over to you, Doc," he told him the other day. This drew a chuckle from Dr. Nederlander, adding to Albert's depression. Why, he asked himself anew, do I insist on playing these sessions for laughs, milking them for applause?

Dr. Nederlander is, you might say, the family psychiatrist. That is, Skippy Mountjoy, Violet's first husband, was the first to go to him; Skippy recommended him to Violet; she, in turn, prevailed upon Albert to see him. Emily *almost* saw him on three occasions: the first time she didn't have anything to wear; the second, she had, but it wasn't dry yet; the third broken appointment had something to do with hundreds of split ends. Violet, who is unhappy in love, goes twice a week; Albert once; Skippy, who is on welfare and has a drinking problem, intermittently. Dr. Nederlander considers their interlocking sorrows high above West End. When he's running late, Albert gazes out his smutty windows at the Cimmerian prospect of the avenue or takes down German paperbacks—mysteries, largely, in translation—from his shelves and blows the dust off them.

When Albert began going to Dr. Nederlander, he assumed Skippy no longer went. After Albert learned that Skippy was still a patient of sorts—asking to be squeezed in when he had overslept and it was too late to get a job running sandwiches from the Leonard Street employment agency he patronized—Albert put it to Dr. Nederlander.

"In effect, I'm subsidizing Skippy," he said, raising himself from the languid pose on the couch he usually adopts. (When Violet goes, Dr. Nederlander sits on the couch, she in the chair. Albert doesn't know Skippy's seating arrangement.)

"He has Medicaid," Dr. Nederlander said.

"But you couldn't afford to see the Skippys of this world unless you had patients like me at forty bucks a pop."

"You are covered under your wife's noncontributory major medical, which pays seventy-five percent of covered charges after a cash deductible of three hundred and fifty dollars."

"Up to a maximum of thirty-five hundred dollars in any twelve-consecutive-month period, and you only get twenty dollars an hour from Medicaid."

"But your tax dollars provide social services for innumerable unfortunates."

Albert whipped off his shirt. "Look at that," he said, indicating eruptions on his shoulders.

Dr. Nederlander put on his reading glasses. "Do you want me to recommend a good dermatologist," he said, "or are you suggesting that I compare you to Job?"

"What I'm suggesting is that no one I know pays for even a *percentage* of his wife's first husband's psychotherapy."

"As we've elicited in previous sessions, your life has become circumscribed. You should widen your circle of friends."

WHAT made Albert think that Violet's love life might have changed for the better was her singing "The Star-Spangled Banner" at a Knicks–Bucks game. At the Garden, Albert sits on the aisle; she is to his left; the flag hangs on their right. Therefore, when they rise for the national anthem and turn to face the flag, she is behind him. On the occasion in question, Albert heard an unfamiliar voice raised in song. After a few bars, he realized it was Violet's. Although they have been married ten years, this was the first time he ever heard her sing "The Star-Spangled Banner"; in fact, he can't recall her singing anything. (In her defense, Violet says she has so sung lots of songs in Albert's hearing, not least "Happy Birthday" on a number of his birthdays. Be that as it may, her voice was foreign to him, pleasing, but slightly flat.)

When Albert said his wife was unhappy in love, you naturally assumed he was responsible. Not in this case—though, in all fairness, more than a few of her woes can be laid at his doorstep. (Forgive me if I picture them as an accumulation of copies of the New York *Times*.) No, for once someone named Owen, a New Realist she met at a film-making class at the New School, let her down.

Albert learned of his existence—and her inconstancy—in Florida. "Neither of you has any emotional content," Violet told him there. "Dr. Nederlander said I shouldn't put all my eggs in one basket. What he didn't tell me was not to put all my eggs in *two* baskets." At the time of this revelation, they were standing up to their waists in the Gulf of Mexico, a setting more conducive to sympathy than hard feelings. All the same, Albert felt that if he spread his feet any farther apart he would be able to detect the earth's curve. (While in this position Albert was put in mind of the fact that his two favorite odors are those of seas and books. If you bury your nose in the gutter of a new book, preferably a paperback, you can detect the mustiness to come; seas are best smelled when cold—no more than sixty-five degrees—and dead calm and with your nose a quarter inch from the surface. If you inhale deeply enough you can smell unseen fishes. Since my aim, here as elsewhere, is to increase understanding, it must be admitted that this hasn't been scientifically determined. Certain fishermen, however, claim to be able to distinguish the aroma of flowering diatoms, which indicates the presence of schools of bluefish. They say the odor resembles that of "a crate of honeydew melons" or of an unspecified amount of "moist cucumbers.")

In New York, Violet once told Albert, "I don't like the relationships in my life." This, evidently, was a further response to his offer to help her lay the Persian rugs that had come back from Spotless that morning—a proposal she had rejected, saying, "I don't want to put them down with you. All you want to do with me are domestic things."

"Of which relationships are you speaking?" Albert asked.

"All of them. They're too bland, too wispy, too elusive."

"Do you mean elusive or allusive?"

"I don't *know*," she wailed. "Could I mean *both* of them?"

Since they were in bed at the time, and the children were presumably asleep, having abandoned the imaginary electric guitars with which, disposed about the living room like statuary in an Italian garden, they accompany the Stones, he drew her to him.

Getting back to the Knicks game, Albert could think of nothing to make Violet break into song—even the national anthem—except that Owen had called or that she had distributed her eggs more prudently. Albert offers in evidence Exhibit A, she took up ice-skating; and Exhibit B, she took up peace-marching. Once or twice a week she announces she's going ice-skating. Upon her return she regales Albert with such tales as that the rink was mobbed with hundreds of *yeshiva buchers* gliding solemnly about in crocheted, beaded, even suède yarmulkes. (It is, no doubt, uncharitable to imagine a window being flung open in a third-floor loft in SoHo, the New Realist shouting down to the street, "You forgot your goddam skates!") Not long ago, she told Albert she was going to Washington for a peace march. "Look for me on television," she said. Albert watched on and off, but didn't see her. "I was there," she said when she got back. "If you had spotted me, you would have seen me give my secret signal."

The cease-fire agreement terminated the marches, but Albert assumes she will keep on skating into summer, when the crowds will thin. He pictures her at last, idly tracing an outside backward eight on the empty rink—a figure well beyond her capability. It is a scene he associates with that of his dad standing at a hotel-room sink, hands underwater, dreamily kneading his beloved garments of sixty-five percent polyester, thirty-five percent cotton.

My dad! Albert exclaims to himself, as much in awe as regret. A few days ago Albert paid him a visit to see how he was holding up against the Oriental tide. A firm named Fukuoka Foto now occupied the office alongside his—the corridor branches to the right at his office—so, in effect, he was cut off. He was at his desk when Albert came in, eyes nearly shut, head fractionally back; the impression was that he was sniffing the air for traces of simmering sukiyaki. The light in his office was dim, the source for most of it being the window behind him, so that when he arose at Albert's entrance he was nearly silhouetted. He seemed much thinner, eroded; he looked, in fact, like the somber coastal formation known as a stack.

Albert's dad asked Albert whether he had come from the

Y. Albert said he had. Albert's dad asked Albert whether anyone had bumped into him while he was swimming and if so what Albert had said to him. They've had this conversation a number of times. Albert said they now let women into the pool on Mondays, Wednesdays, and Fridays, and what he had told her was, "You know, you're being anti-social."

"Many years ago," Albert's dad said, "I worked on a chicken farm in New Jersey. Jews, you know, have an affinity for all phases of the poultry business. When I fed the chickens, I would inadvertently step on their toes. I said, 'Excuse me.' "

Albert's dad's utterances usually have a high moral content.

They sat in silence for a bit, the gloom abruptly thickening as the sun passed behind a cloud or office building. Albert thought of pulling the chain on the standing lamp by his chair; then it occurred to him that the bulbs might have long since burnt out. He was tempted to take off his shirt and show his dad the eruptions, but that would have meant launching into a greatly revised account of the last ten years of his life, and his dad wouldn't put up with the *vie romanisée* he fobs off on Dr. Nederlander. "I have more at stake," Albert's dad would say.

"Many years ago," he started anew (he gets on these kicks, Albert reflected, his voice nearly entering the head register, as though he were speaking to him from the other side), "there used to be a place in the Bronx called Starlight Park—"

"Where in the Bronx?"

"What conceivable difference does it make? You know nothing of the Bronx. To you, it's terra incognita." Albert's dad often accuses Albert of being indifferent to his, Albert's dad's, past. "You have a habit of asking questions to hear yourself speak."

"I go days without speaking," Albert told him.

"In Starlight Park," Albert's dad went on, "there was a vast outdoor swimming pool. It was a hundred yards long—"

"A hundred yards!"

"A hundred. Seventy-five. It was vast. One summer, when I was a young man, I would go there every day to play handball. When I was through I would jump in the pool at its deepest point, expel all of my breath, and lie on my back on the bottom with my arms outspread—"

He tilted back in his chair, held his arms out wide, and gazed—Albert would say beatifically, Albert's dad would say momentarily—at the ceiling.

"—and look up."

As for me, Albert muses, looking down is my fate or forte: at women's foreheads gleaming in the dark, as I mentioned earlier; at the sidewalk to see where I'm going or, as Dr. Nederlander would say, where I've been; at the pages of a book, as at this moment.

" 'When thou at the random grim forge, powerful amidst peers/ Didst fettle for the great grey drayhorse his bright and battering sandal!' " Albert intones to a woman who has lost her husband in Vietnam, while his pathetic little bundle of laundry flies about in one of the Sans Souci dryers.

People are stirred differently, too, although—and this perplexed Marx—literature depends on and resounds with common chords. For example, Dr. Johnson contended that no poetical passage rivalled the description of the temple in

"The Mourning Bride"—"How reverend is the face of this tall pile . . ." Of course, he wasn't trying to get into the pants of the Sans Souci clientele.

"I know I've bumped into you before somewhere, you know," the widow says as Albert closes his book.

In his motel room, when they've undressed, he lies on his back on the carpet and says, "Hold my legs."

"There?" she says.

"No. The ankles."

"Here?"

"But really clamp down on them. Put your weight behind it."

"You know, I hope you're not into heavy S & M, you know."

"I know. It's just that I forgot to do my sit-ups."

When they are in bed, Albert gets a collect call from Emily. "Next Tuesday is the third anniversary of the day I met Sean," she informs Albert, "and I'm getting him a mist-type styler and I wondered if you wanted to make a contribution."

Brimming with love, Albert pledges five dollars.

A moment later, the phone rings again. Will Albert accept a collect call from a Mr. Mountjoy in New York?

"I will not."

"In that case, I'll pay for it, operator," Albert hears Skippy say.

"Don't believe him," Albert says. "He hasn't got a dime to his name. He's on welfare. I have to contribute toward his psychotherapy."

"What number are you calling from?" the operator asks Skippy.

He reels off one that is strangely familiar to Albert, being his own. He pictures Skippy lolling about on his bed, negligently unbuttoning his collar, loosening a hand-blocked foulard Albert wore before he was married—Violet slips Skippy Albert's old clothes. Albert supposes there is comfort in the fact that they wear different sizes.

"If it wouldn't be putting too much of a strain on our relationship," Skippy says, "I was wondering whether, as a fellow-citizen of the Republic of Letters, you could see your way clear to wiring me twenty to get my typewriter out of hock. I'm in the middle of a sonnet sequence."

"Use a pen," Albert says. "Like Shelley."

Albert hangs up and flings himself upon the widow, as though executing a racing dive. You know, he thinks, I *have* bumped into her before, in the pool at the Y. Albert keeps this discovery to himself; he doesn't mean to have his life veer into the novelistic. In addition, he prays that she won't, like a nineteenth-century heroine, remember and cherish him as she unrolls each pair of children's socks they rolled together in the Sans Souci Launderama, he pining the while for the little, lost feet of his stepchildren. Albert reflects that his life has become increasingly like a dream from which he has less and less expectation of awakening.

After she has gone, Albert lights a pipe, takes up the "Manyōshū"—in translation—and resumes reading where he left off the night before. Cuckoos, plum blossoms, and pessimism imbue his mind. His forehead is peeling. As he absently rubs it, bits of dead skin drift down pathetically, like blossoms, or airy snow, or ash. At the same time, the smoke from his pipe rises like that from salt fires. It is vain, he muses, to expect the smoke to bear his skin upward. He would like to compare the sound of turning pages with some natural effect, but none comes to mind.

A FEW days later, Albert is in a Boston whaler, off Nonesuch, on the edge of the deep, watching shearwaters migrating from Tristan da Cunha to the Newfoundland Banks. They come singly, by and large, greaters mostly, with the odd Manx, ranging deviously down the wave troughs, as though searching for something. Albert fancies it is remembered fragments of their pasts. After all, they had come this way before. Perhaps they recall me from other springs, Albert reflects, bobbing here, Jewish in bearing—that is, somewhat hunched—but younger, more slender, but no less full of wonder.

Like the acrobats, usually related, who form human pillars by standing upon one another's shoulders, as we grow older, heavier, less agile, we take our place farther down until, at last, we are at the bottom, supporting the rest. There we totter about—a bit theatrically from time to time, Albert admits.

FOUR

~~~~~~~~~~~~~~~~~~~~~~~~~

On the flight to Miami, Albert wins a bottle of wine for producing the oldest penny. In case you haven't flown lately, stewardesses now play games with passengers. Albert hadn't entered into the spirit of the thing. For years his dad has exhorted him to do just that—enter into the spirit of things. What a nice ring it has, Albert has come to realize; it might almost be the name of a Victorian pastime —Entering Into the Spirit of Things. Gazing down at the smoldering Everglades, he imagines the rollicksome Marxes playing it during a picnic on Hampstead Heath.

Albert hadn't expected to win; the penny he grudgingly dug out of his pocket was dated 1945. When, in its final approach, the plane enters a pall of smoke, Albert dwells on the vanity of human wishes, which his dad has had more luck impressing on him.

The girl behind the counter at the car-rental office on North Le Jeune is wearing a miniskirt. As she turns to get a form, Albert notices that the insides of her thighs jiggle, and he is mildly aroused.

"Do you and your husband like wine?" he says, flourishing the bottle and setting it on the counter.

"I'm not married," she says, "but I enjoy it in moderation."

Albert shifts his glance. Beyond a plate glass window rows of brightly colored Novas and Dusters gleam in the sun; they might have been tesserae in a great composition of which he could not see enough to grasp or which he was viewing from the wrong angle. Such is often the case. Although his dad doesn't know how to drive, he must have passed this way, proselyting, Albert concludes, for once you entered into the spirit of things, you enjoyed them in moderation. "You're forever going to extremes," his dad has told Albert. His tone suggested that this was some malarial coast Albert insisted on visiting without taking the requisite shots.

Albert feels his desire for the rent-a-car girl waning; if he is going to sleep with her he will have to talk to her, and he has lost interest in the story of his life. Whatever the rewards, being compelled to relate it yet again seems as much of an intrusion as fishing out his pennies had been.

"Then permit me to give it to you," Albert says, presenting the bottle with both hands, like a wine steward, so she can read the undistinguished label. As he does so, it occurs to him that this is the way infants are held up to view. He himself must have been displayed thus. He imagines a giant hand under his bottom, another supporting his head, his dad gazing critically down at him. Had he proved satisfactory?

Albert reflects that as his dad has grown older—he is now seventy-seven—he has become more lavish in his praise, at least that which he bestows on his surviving compeers. Where once he would refer to someone as "a wonderful guy" he now extolls him as "a warm and delightful human being." Although such citations had the virtue of being slightly more specific, they had the defect of sounding like the first drafts of eulogies. Indeed, his dad is in great demand these days as a eulogist. "I have finally found my true calling," he told Albert. "You couldn't have done it without your friends, relatives, and associates," Albert told his dad. "No, I couldn't have done it *with* them," he said. A warm and witty human being.

Albert often attends the services at which his dad is asked to say a few words. From his seat on the highly varnished bench, Albert admires how well his dad carries his years. Instead of being bent, shrivelled, diminished, his clothes hanging about him like a sack, he seems more erect, fit, spruce, as though he is streamlining himself to make his own impending ascent to Heaven as rapid and frictionless as possible.

Afterwards, mingling with the mourners on the sidewalk outside the chapel, Albert invariably finds himself comparing the scene to the intermission of a play, and once or twice he has caught himself straining to hear the bell summoning them back for the next act. There has to be a greater resolution.

Morton Savoy, D.D.S. is usually among the last to disperse. "I guess I better be drifting off," is what he always says. Albert has the impression that each successive destination in Uncle Morty's life holds less in store and wonders when he had arrived at the turning point; further, if this is a general rule, whether he, Albert, will be able to recognize his. A gentle and painstaking soul, as Albert's dad has lately termed him, Uncle Morty is his mother's and father's dentist as well. Albert has been going to him all his life, his appointments increasingly taking on a melancholy cast; the water that perpetually runs around the basin into which he rinses now has a Stygian gurgle. Each time he lies submissively in the chair, Albert remarks anew that Uncle Morty has aged more conventionally than his dad; that is, every six months he is smaller, except for his feet. These remain the same size but appear larger by contrast, giving him a spurious stability. If this trend continues, Albert speculates, all that will be left for his dad to eulogize will be a pair of shoes.

In consequence of their respective positions, Albert feels that he and Uncle Morty are like lovers engaged in a long, unbroken, dispassionate affair. As he worked on his teeth through the years, Uncle Morty's face hovered intently over Albert's; Albert knows it perhaps better than Violet's, and sympathetically has marked its changes.

Pursuing this theme, Albert concludes that such an intimate relationship would be more appropriate if Dr. Nederlander were the other principal, but they sit ten feet apart, Albert at point "A," with his chair inclined toward Dr. Nederlander's at an angle of 53° from the imaginary base line "b" running between Dr. Nederlander's chair and his; Dr. Nederlander at point "N," with his chair inclined toward Albert's at an angle of 47° from "b." If they were willing to turn their heads so that their eyes might meet, their lines of sight—"a" and "n"—would intersect at point "C."

After Albert had gone to Dr. Nederlander for a month, he asked Violet to find "C" for him.

Violet's Calculations

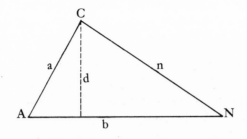

given: b = 10 feet
$$\angle A = 53°$$
$$\angle N = 47°$$
$$\angle C = 180° - (53° + 47°) = 180° - 100° = 80°$$

Applying the laws of sines,
$$\frac{a}{\sin \angle A} = \frac{b}{\sin \angle C}$$
$$\frac{a}{\sin 53°} = \frac{10}{\sin 80°}$$

From the table of functions,
$$\sin 53° = .7986$$
$$\sin 80° = .9848$$
$$\therefore \quad \frac{a}{.7986} = \frac{10}{.9848}$$
$$.9848 \, a = 7.986$$
$$a \frac{7.986}{.9848} = \underline{\underline{8.109}}$$

Now we can find d:
$$\sin 47° = \frac{d}{a}$$
$$\sin 47° = .7314$$
$$.7314 = \frac{d}{8.109}$$
$$d = 8.109 \, (.7314) = \underline{\underline{5.9309}} \text{ feet}$$

She determined it was located at an unspecified height above an unravelling Oriental carpet 5.9309 feet from Albert. However, both Dr. Nederlander and Albert invariably turn to more or less gaze at each other, but Albert turns more than Dr. Nederlander since he is paying and wants to get his money's worth.

Albert always thought he knew where he stood—or sat— with Uncle Morty, but the last time he went to him for a perio, Uncle Morty was wearing a cerise coat. "You look like a hair stylist," Albert said.

"My colleagues felt we should be 'with it,'" Uncle Morty said fatalistically. Since his practice had declined, he had given up his office on Amsterdam and now shared a suite on Central Park South with three younger men. "Do you know how to floss?"

"Up to now I didn't even know it was a verb," Albert said.

Uncle Morty tore off a length of dental floss and held it up critically, nearly at arm's length, much, Albert thought, as his dad would display one of his mom's hairs after finding it in the bathroom sink. "Wind it around your middle finger," he said. "Did I say tight? You're not supposed to cut off the circulation."

Albert pictured himself in ten years with all of his teeth, but minus the first joints of his middle fingers. "Before we go any further, Uncle Morty," he said, "I want to tell you that if it requires a high degree of eye-hand coordination, I'm not going to be a very good flosser."

"You're snapping the floss, Albert," Uncle Morty said. "You're not supposed to snap the floss."

"Is there no room for individual expression in flossing?"

"It's not an art form," Uncle Morty said.

Neither, Albert decides a week or two later, parting the drapes, is the process of restoration, be the object a cast-iron building or a human relationship, as his mom trustingly calls it. The scene is lurid, unexpected. "Sunrise on the Charles." These words come to mind—Albert finds himself silently articulating them—as though he is reading them off a plate below the view, which his eyes have sought. This reaction is undoubtedly a result of the prospect being framed by the window and by his not immediately being able to make out what is before him—a common enough failing. Bands of garish reds, dark indefinite masses evoke a milieu more exotic than Back Bay—indeed, one suggestive of the Near East. Subject matter has less to do with this illusion than coloring, rendering. The effect is primitive, or inept, and strongly reminiscent of the gaudy rugs depicting floral arrangements, kittens, the Last Supper peddled by Lebanese Jews. Reality imposes itself. Beneath Albert's gaze the reds pale, diffuse, the water begins to move, and he succumbs to thoughts of Messianism, a life lived in deferment.

He lets the drapes close and glances down at the bed. Amanda Moran is sleeping along the near edge, as she had been when he stole out of her bedroom ten or twelve years earlier—anyway, before he got married. Suppose she hasn't stirred since, Albert reflects, peering at her face, which has agreeably aged in the interval, like an old apple. His attention is next drawn to two strands of dental floss dangling from his middle fingers. The whereabouts of the other ends is not evident; they might be clews, extending far into the past. Attempting to unravel the floss, Albert recalls being fairly drunk and naked in front of Amanda's medicine cabinet mirror the night before, remorsefully flossing. As he payed out the floss from one finger and took it up on another, he had the inexact impression that he was raising anchor at last—or was he letting more chain down?

"What precisely are you up to in there?" she had called from the bedroom.

"I'm carefully following an effective personal oral hygiene program."

"At 3 A.M.?"

"Amanda, I'm on plaque control . . . Holy shit!"

"Albert, what happened?"

"It broke."

"Come here, baby. I'll tie a knot."

Albert stumbled from the bathroom, trailing the floss behind him.

Now he removes Amanda's cats from his clothes and gets dressed. He lets the floss be and begins plucking cat hairs off his suit. I'll have to get it cleaned, he thinks, or Violet will suspect something.

He notices that Amanda's eyes are open and obligingly approaches her. "See you in ten years," he says.

"Albert, we can't go on meeting like this," she says, reaching out to embrace him or to remove an additional hair.

If Violet has tumbled, Albert muses as they drive along the Rickenbacker Causeway to see the afterglow over Biscayne Bay, she hasn't let on. Albert esteems the afterglow as viewed from the causeway, as does Violet. To see it in all its glory from a moving vehicle requires split-second timing, however. According to Violet's calculations— Albert once told his dad he had a calculating wife, whereupon his dad quoted Benjamin Constant: "Jokes appear to hold the real key to life"—on this particular evening they

have to be crossing Bay Bridge, the best vantage point, at
6:12 and it is now 6:10 and Bear Cut Bridge is not yet in
sight. It's going to be dicey. The speed limit on the causeway is 45 m.p.h. and they have 2.2 miles to go before reaching the midpoint of Bay Bridge. Violet says that if Albert
cranks her up to 66.96 m.p.h. and holds her there, he'll hit
it right on the nose.

Violet's Calculations

Acceleration, '70 Vega

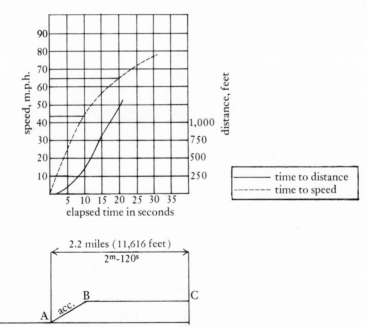

To obtain minimum constant speed between
B and C, acceleration has to be at a maximum.
Ideally, instantaneous constant speed, then,
would be between A and C at

$$\frac{2.2 \times 60}{2} = 66 \text{ m.p.h.}$$

· *49* ·

CONSTANT ACCELERATION
S = distance moved in feet
V_f = final velocity (feet per second)
V_o = initial velocity (feet per second)
a = acceleration (feet per second $\times$ second)
t = time of acceleration in seconds

CONSTANT VELOCITY
S = distance moved
V = velocity
t = time of motion

ACCELERATION

$$S = \frac{(V_f + V_o)t}{2}$$

$$a = \frac{V_f - V_o}{t}$$

According to ordinates, time elapsed
between 45 m.p.h. and 66 m.p.h. is 10 seconds

$$\text{Acceleration} = \frac{(V_f - V_o)}{t}$$

$$a = \frac{V_{66} - V_{45}}{10} = \frac{(66 \times 1.467) - (45 \times 1.467)}{10}$$

$$\frac{96.82 - 66.01}{10} = \boxed{3.081 \frac{ft^2}{s}}$$

$$S = \frac{(V_f + V_o)t}{2} = \frac{(96.82 + 66.01) \times 10^5}{2} =$$

814.15 feet

DISTANCE AT CONSTANT SPEED
11,616 − 814.15 = 10,801.85
TIME AT CONSTANT SPEED
120 − 10 = 110 seconds
LOWEST POSSIBLE SPEED

$$\frac{10,801.85}{110} = 98.2 \frac{ft.}{s}$$

$$98.2 \times .6818 = \boxed{66.96 \text{ m.p.h.}}$$

Smoothly accelerating, Albert briefs Violet. His area of responsibility is to maintain speed, hers is to keep an eye out for the law.

Events happen thick and fast.

18:10.23. *Violet*: Cop car at two o'clock.

18:10.47. *Police Officer*: Where's the fire?

18:10.50. *Albert*: Beyond the rim of the world.

18:10.54. *Violet* (sotto voce): Holy shit!

18:10.57. *Police Officer* (to Albert): Prosify that, Jack.

18:11.01. *Albert*: We're late for the afterglow, officer! We've got to be at Bay Bridge by 6:12!

18:11.17. *Police Officer* (glancing at his watch): Wind 'er up and follow me.

He gets back in his cruiser, turns on the cherry light and the siren, and shoots off the shoulder, his rear wheels tossing shell. Drafting behind him, Albert and Violet flash across Bay Bridge at 92 m.p.h., catching the afterglow at the moment of its greatest refulgence.

They park alongside the cruiser in the grove of Australian pines before West Bridge and watch the sky become drained of color and evenly darken, the bay lose its gilding —processes one would have thought would take years. The police officer tells them he is enrolled in Imaginative Writing at Miami-Dade Junior College, and presses on Albert a sheaf of poems. These he keeps in the glove compartment to rework by map light while the tires of unapprehended speeders sing in the night.

It strikes Albert that while the police officer was counting feet he had been struggling to count sheep. As with so much else, Albert has come late in life to this anodyne and has failed to master it. (Among other things he has taken up after forty with one degree of diffidence or another are adultery and loving his wife.) The first part is easy: an empty meadow. This he has no difficulty envisioning. In fact, he dallies there, enjoying the lowering prospect, which is executed in the manner of Philip de Koninck. The fence presents a problem. How is it put together? Albert has a lively imagination, a middling background in Western art, but he's not handy. When he was in the third grade, his shop teacher wrote on his report card: "Albert has good intentions, but insufficient manual dexterity to carry them out." (He's come to realize that as a moral agent, he's all thumbs, too.) He has tried erecting a number of fences in his mind, but the business of fitting the rails into the posts defeated him. His rickety creations would, he feared, collapse if more than one bobolink sat on them. At last, he threw tradition to the winds and stapled barbed wire to the posts. The first sheep—Albert knows sheep; Giotto did terrific sheep—approached the fence and leapt over. Its leg action didn't seem right. For the next sheep, he altered it. This time he realized that what was bothering him was what the hind legs did when the front hooves struck the ground. Sheep *have* hooves, don't they? He considered borrowing a Hulcher and shooting a couple of rolls of Josh jumping over a footstool, so he could analyze the disposition of his limbs. Meanwhile, the third sheep refused the jump. Perhaps he had made the fence too high.

At this juncture, he realized he didn't know enough about sheep vis-à-vis fences. He called the American Sheep Producers Association, which put him on to a major sheep owner, a sheepherder, and a retired "camp jack" who came to the phone in the lounge of DuWayne's Bowl-O-Drome & Recreation on U.S. 70 south of Richfield, Utah, where he was drinking tomato juice and beer. From those sources he learned the following: Contrary to the familiar representations, for the most part sheep won't jump fences unless they are urged to do so by man or are stirred up by a predator. This rule of thumb applies to range sheep rather than farm flocks; the latter, of course, are more docile. However, even a range sheep isn't usually obsessed with escaping from an enclosure unless pressured, and a sheep would much rather break through a fence or find a hole in it than jump over it. For this reason, most sheepmen use "L-wood" fences, which have close wire squares instead of horizontal strands of wire. The fences contain about three feet of these squares, topped with two or three barbed-wire strands, making a four-foot barrier in all. A sheep can jump from two and a half to three feet. They have pretty good explosive power (standing jump), but generally take a little run at the fence. Sheep follow a leader. If, under pressure, one sheep jumps a fence, the others will follow, but rarely in single file. They will almost always jump simultaneously. The only way sheep would line up and jump over a fence one at a time, as customarily envisioned, would be if a leader, usually under pressure, jumped the fence and there wasn't room for the others to clear it en masse.

Albert relates his findings to Dr. Nederlander, who nods several times. "Dr. Nederlander is the only man I know who is more inexpressive than you," Violet has told Albert. "But he may be concealing his true feelings for therapeutic reasons." Nodding and allowing his eyes to close is Dr. Nederlander's entire repertory, and since at least two of the four bulbs in his ceiling fixture—in whose plate a prize collection of dead insects is on permanent exhibition—are always out, his responses seem even more minimal, more shrouded.

Bringing his head to a halt, Dr. Nederlander says, "The sheep, Albert, drop them. Try a more urban situation. Conceptualize, possibly seriatim, Bradley running his man into that double screen and getting free for the baseline jumper."

Dr. Nederlander's passions and Albert's converge at two points: the Knicks and food. In a previous decade, Amanda Moran had told Albert that on the basis of sleeping with a random sample of Jews, she had determined that their racial disquiet was food-oriented, centering around applesauce. "Your ingestion is symptomatic of your limitations," Dr. Nederlander once said to Albert. "You have almost infinitely postponed the achievement of pleasure. Deli, Albert, is a backwater in the tide of Western civilization."

Subsequent to his advice *in re* the sheep, Dr. Nederlander closes his eyes for a longer period than usual, giving Albert the opportunity to study his eyelids, which in the half-light seem unnaturally smooth, marmoreal, nearly heroic in scale.

When Dr. Nederlander reopens his eyes, Albert tells him that it so happens that after dinner Violet and he are going to a Knicks game, and that he will watch Bradley closely so he can get that move down pat.

For the first time since Albert has known him, Dr. Nederlander gives evidence of being in the grip of a moderately deep emotion. He even passes a hand over his spacious brow, and when he speaks his voice is more vibrant than customary.

"Tonight," he says, "eat Chinese."

As it turns out, Albert goes to see the Knicks with Barney, who is now eighteen. They eat at the Stage.

The game goes into double overtime and is unbearably tense.

"I'm not going to look if we shoot any fouls," Albert tells Barney. "I'm going to close my eyes."

"I'll tell you what happens," Barney says.

"Don't tell me," Albert pleads. "I don't want to hear the truth."

"Give me your hand," Barney says, taking it and placing it on his thigh, "I'll tap it if the shot is good."

Gianelli is fouled. As he approaches the line, Albert shuts his eyes and listens to the crowd grow silent. More time passes than he would expect. Has Gianelli in fact missed? Albert thinks: Wouldn't I have been able to tell by the reaction of the fans? As the silence continues, he imagines the game is over and that everybody has left the Garden but Barney and he. Barney's finger strikes his hand. Albert doesn't want to open his eyes, but to sit in the dark in the midst of the howling crowd, his hand on Barney's thigh.

In this respect, Albert recalls Violet telling him how she had sat for hours by her father's hospital bed when he was dying, her hand in his. From all signs, he was unconscious, but when she fiercely whispered in his ear, "I'm Violet; if you know it's me, squeeze my hand," he would squeeze it.

What follows is tender and complicated. Violet awakens Albert in what lately has become known as his room, Violet having moved into Emily's room when she went to stay with Sean's family in Nebraska, which meant that Sean's mother had to move in with his father. Albert sees his stepdaughter as a sort of Clotho, twisting here, untwisting there to maintain a mysterious symmetry.

On the morning in question—it is morning because Albert's room is perceptibly lightening, as though his bed is being raised through the high interior of the sea—Violet enters, crouches by Albert's ear, and whispers, "I can't tie my tie."

She holds out a plaid necktie of the size they had bought Barney in the boys' department at Brooks years ago; it might well be one of his: an example of what the Japanese call *mono no aware*, the poignancy of things. Albert props himself up on his pillows, puts the tie about her neck, and attempts to knot it. After several failures, he asks her to sit on the edge of the bed, with her back to him. Putting his arms around her, he ties the tie. In much the same way, he recalls, when Barney had asked him to part his hair, he made Barney stand with his back to him and bow his head. As Albert gently tightens the knot about Violet's throat, he thinks that they were never as close, as allied in purpose. As though she were prey to similar sentiments she says, "Why don't you talk about something important with Dr. Nederlander? All you talk about is growing old."

She means I omit sex, Albert thinks as he walks along the forbidding perspective of West End Avenue at midday in the company of Dulcie Barclay, whom he hasn't seen for ten or eleven years. They are on their way to the apartment of a friend of hers who is skiing in Courchevel. The ostensible purpose of the visit is for Dulcie to collect her friend's mail. The actual purpose is to have a nooner.

"This is it," Dulcie says, taking Albert's hand and leading him into a lobby evidently designed by an admirer of Balthasar Neumann. Many a time has Albert gazed up at its soaring stuccoes, sculptures, and frescoes—the whole *Gesamtkunstwerk*: It is Dr. Nederlander's building. The doorman, a greybeard who isn't on when Albert sees Dr. Nederlander, approaches. Albert wonders: Is he going to offer to serve as a guide to the lobby's splendors, or is it his portion to play an admonitory role, like Wordsworth's leech-gatherer? He stands respectfully before them, his dark uniform, upon which the piping has all but unravelled, as shiny as carbon paper. Dulcie asks for her friend's mail. The doorman retires into a murky, chapel-like recess. When he returns with the pile of mail, carrying it with both hands as if it were a relic whose keeping he is about to entrust to her, he tells her that the maid is "up there."

"The maid?" Albert says as he and Dulcie rise in the elevator. "What's the maid doing up there if she's in Courchevel?"

"She doesn't want to lose her," Dulcie says. "And if she's going to keep paying her while she's away, she might as well give her something to do so she can get her money's worth."

By this time they are in the corridor, and Dulcie is fitting a key to a lock.

"Like what?" Albert persists.

"Like cleaning the stove," she says, opening the door, "or doing the drapes."

Indeed, over Dulcie's shoulder, Albert glimpses the maid, enveloped in a flowered house dress, standing on the radiator cover at one of the living-room windows, about to take down a Fortuny drape—or possibly, putting it up; they don't stay long enough for Albert to learn which.

"But doesn't she come on certain days?" he says as they go down in the elevator.

"I can never remember which are her ones," Dulcie says.

Albert studies the demotic avowals of love scratched on the elevator walls. What have they been done with? House keys? Human nails? Wordsworthian dim sadness and blind thoughts he dispels. If I can't look at my life as farcical, he thinks, I can't look at it—like a double overtime.

"I think my life is more prefigured than most," he says to Dulcie.

"I think the only life that interests you is your own," Dulcie says.

"Admittedly," Albert says. "But, as Constant said, 'only faintly.'"

Recrossing the lobby, Albert glances up at the ceiling and imagines his dad, with Merit in tow, arms tightly pressed to his sides, speed lines indicating his great velocity, flashing by mildly astonished cherubim en route to the empyrean.

Albert says to Dr. Nederlander the next time he sees him, "I'm almost positive the maid was Violet."

Dr. Nederlander makes no response. Only one bulb is burning overhead. Albert can hear, but not well enough to make out what it is, the classical music Dr. Nederlander pipes into his waiting room to drown out his patients' secrets and sorrows—or to provide an accompaniment for them. Unresistingly, Albert and Dr. Nederlander fall to discussing restaurants. Dr. Nederlander recommends a little French place in the West Forties. "It's not first-rate," he says, "but it's honest, and the price is right. May I suggest the cassoulet."

Albert gets up to leave. When he opens the double doors to Dr. Nederlander's office—in between which he has imagined that a very thin and determined lunatic could secrete himself—he is struck by the force of the music, a Handel organ concerto. The waiting room is empty, as it always is. Sometimes Albert fancies that Violet and he are Dr. Nederlander's only patients. Taking it a step further, Albert sometimes wonders if *she* actually goes.

Dr. Nederlander is saying something. "I can't hear you," Albert says, turning on the threshold.

"Bring money!" Dr. Nederlander shouts above the sonorities. "They don't honor credit cards."

EMILY calls collect. She and Sean are en route to Florida to look for work in boutiques. "Do you know if Florida still makes women wear bathing caps in swimming pools?" she asks Albert plaintively.

"It was my impression that they would turn back if the law was enforced," Albert tells his dad as they walk around the reservoir. "The fate of Western civilization is balanced on self-indulgence, socio-economically speaking."

"Marx had occasion to refer to his life's work as 'Ökonomische drek,' " his dad says, lengthening his stride.

Why does he always make me bust my hump to keep up, Albert wonders.

LYRICALLY flossing in the Beverly Sunset Hotel early one morning, Albert recalls his dad on the cinder path, vigorously swinging his arms, hellbent for the vanishing point. Albert's pajama top is held together by three disparate safety pins. (As he mentioned to Dr. Nederlander, Violet no longer sews his buttons, to which Dr. Nederlander responded that although it is not his practice to reveal confidences, Violet has already brought it up, that he is fed up to here with this button *drek*, and that Albert should address himself to the wellsprings of his pain.) The bathroom window is open and an unidentified bird is singing in the garden below. Albert grows aware that he is more or less manipulating the floss in time with the bird's heartsore measures.

Putting his raincoat over his pajamas, he descends to the

garden, in which winding paths lead to pink stucco bunga-
lows, and tracks the bird to the top of a tall, unidentified
tree; what Albert *has* come to grips with is that he is an
ignoramus west of the Rockies. As he is jotting down the
bird's field marks in a notebook, a voice says, "All right,
hold it right there."

Albert looks over his shoulder at a security man with a
drawn gun.

"Hands against the bungalow, Jack," he adds. To comply
without stepping in a flower bed, Albert has to assume
much the same angle that his chair is inclined toward Dr.
Nederlander's. As he is being frisked, he imagines the
yellowing soles of a daytime game-show host pressed
against the wall opposite his hands to get better purchase
while *schtupping* a bottomless waitress. Just an idea.

Needless to say, the security man turns out to be a bird
watcher and insists on making a Xerox of his place list for
the Beverly Sunset and leaving it in Albert's box at the
front desk.

Albert returns to his room and, taking his suit in his
arms, as though it were an old and undemanding love
partner, stretches out on the bed and idly plucks dog hairs
off it, working from the cuffs up in an attempt to bring to
his life what his dad, despairing, calls "a little order." The
hairs had been shed by Lois Hamilton's spitz, which had
compassionately licked Albert's unoccupied soles while he
embraced its mistress on her kitchen floor. He had last
clapped her to his bosom ten or eleven years before, but
found her little changed, except that she had taken up
gourmet cooking.

In the kitchen on South Mariposa, the fluorescent light
gleaming in the spines of a complete set of Time–Life

cookbooks, Albert had a vision of Amanda, Dulcie, Lois as great, indolent caryatids bearing him submissively upward through time—aerodynamically unsound.

ALBERT invites Dr. Nederlander to a Knicks game. During time-outs he reads to him from a journal he kept at Wellfleet the previous summer.

"Here's a revealing entry," Albert says. " 'July nineteen. I asked Violet to take my picture coming out of Slough Pond after I had swum around it. "But I already took it," she said. "That was *Round* Pond," I said. When I approached the place where I had started, I made her out standing in the shadows of the pines, wearing the gown she had stolen from New York Hospital after her hysterectomy, the Instamatic to her eye. "Don't take it until I'm nearer," I said, striding ashore. "I have the spot picked out," she said. "If I loom any closer I'm not going to be in focus," I said. "Stop," she said. "Unclench your fists." When she had taken my picture, she removed the gown and entered the water. Among the hyacinths I held her face between my palms, squeezing it. "You look like a walnut," I said. "I read your journal," she said. "Was it any good?" I said. "It was like reading love letters addressed to others," she said.' "

The game is in its waning minutes. Dr. Nederlander is hunched forward in his seat, seemingly brooding over the destiny of the tiny figures of the players far below. "That No. 42 is the stiff of the century," he says at last.

Later that night, Albert calls Uncle Morty at home. "Mission to Plaque Control," he says.

"Yes, Albert," Uncle Morty says.

"As I'm speaking to you, I'm holding between my right

thumb and forefinger a gold inlay you cunningly fashioned for me in my youth."

"What is it doing out of your mouth, Albert?"

"It nearly went down the drain, Uncle Morty."

"What precisely have you been up to?"

"Flossing. It flew out of my mouth, describing a parabola. It whizzed around the sink like a roulette ball."

"You're not supposed to take out your rage on your teeth, Albert. Flossing isn't an outlet for repressed violence."

"I have other qualities," Albert says.

BUT I digress. Albert, you recall, was presenting the bottle of wine to the rent-a-car girl. He has held his pose all this while, as has she, as though they are Victorians sitting for a photograph designed to excite strong emotions. Mrs. Cameron's "Pray God, Bring Father Safely Home" and "Seventy Years Ago, My Darling, Seventy Years Ago" come to mind. Now the action flows. She accepts the wine, fills out the rental agreement; he signs and initials in both places, fingers the keys. As he drives over the Rickenbacker Causeway, the sun sets unbeheld behind him.

Several nights later, unable to sleep because of the explosion of colliding shuffleboard discs on the court outside his motel room, Albert turns on the radio and catches the end of a newscast on WFUN: ". . . was killed and five hundred dollars is missing from the Flamingo U-Drive office on North Le Jeune." This is the agency from which he rented the car. Banal but true. Banal *and* true. Truth isn't conditional.

The next couple of days, Albert looks through the newspapers for an account of the crime. There is none. If the girl with the tremulous thighs has been murdered, there certainly would have been one. The victim must have been the elderly black who took his bag and put it in the trunk. These speculations occupy him as he walks on the beach early one morning. It is high water and the sea is as calm as milk in a pail. The high-tide line is festooned with the fuchsia sacs of Portuguese men-of-war. Albert recalls walking with his dad by the Hudson and calling his attention to floating condoms. His dad said they were balloons from waterfront bars. For years Albert had envisioned a fantastic New York in which bars on pilings, decorated with crêpe paper and balloons, as though for a birthday party, lined the shore from the Sixties south. At night, from a boat, you could hear the revelry and dimly make out the roistering patrons crowded at the windows, releasing balloons. One of the great, thematic currents that flows through Albert's life has swept them to sea and deposited them at his feet to point up his dad's rectitude.

In an hour Albert will drive out to Le Jeune. The elderly black will be hosing down the plate glass windows. Within the cascade, the girl will shimmer as in a pointillist painting. Opening the door, raising his voice so he can be heard over the water drumming on the glass, Albert will begin his life story.

When the owl awakens him, he will notice that the base of the lamp on her bedside table is fashioned from the wine bottle. The same owl had awakened Violet and him at Wellfleet. "Did you ever realize that if you had done thus and so, we wouldn't be breaking up?" she had said. The fog was particularly thick. He hadn't answered.

In North Miami, lying beneath a shake roof, hemmed in by crotons, the bedroom reeking of burning brush, Albert will agree with Goethe's remarks on the ending of "Novelle" that a lyrical conclusion was necessary.

Last summer, on the Cape, we heard the same owl
Transmitting its great distressful vowel
From the woods. The same? she said. Not the selfsame,
He said, secretly recounting his wealth of shame.
Slumberous, he wondered if the threefold Os
Transfiguring their connubial woes. . . .

He will falter. Doggerel, like the form and substance of so much of his life. If he had the gift, he would make something of

Suppose it was the identical bird, tracking him down,

rhyming it with

grey silk dressing gown.

That was what the owl's plumage resembled, what his dad had worn years ago, when, upright and mettlesome, he had stood, indistinct, at the threshold of Albert's bedroom, believing Albert to be asleep, and gazed at him with love and terror.

The owl will be perched in a tree hibiscus, chapleted in smoke, listening to the rent-a-car girl's cries—

oh, oh, oh.

And Albert will hear

His dad, the moral scientist, intoning no, no, no.

FIVE

UNABLE TO SLEEP, Albert wanders through his dark apartment. His way is fitfully lit by little flaring lights—static electricity manifested when he touches this or that to get his bearings. The gleams put him in mind of fireflies in remote country lanes and enlarge his sadness by taking it out-of-doors and extending it backward and forward to summer; more of these behind, he acknowledges in line with Philodemos, than ahead. His distress is exacerbated by the notion that his apartment might, in fact, harbor an enfeebled firefly or two, which pathetically emerge at night, perhaps from the recesses of the piano, which is badly out of tune, some notes silent. What was there for them to *eat*? This anxiety he recognizes as a product, or portion, of his Jewish upbringing.

Albert bumps into the couch, which isn't where it was

when he went to bed. He reaches out a hand to steady himself. It comes to rest on the dry billow of the open dictionary. This, too, is in a different place. Albert imagines it creeping secretly in the dark, like a great slug, propelled by the energy generated by the compression of knowledge.

He barges into his wife's room, formerly his step-daughter's. Violet is sitting up in bed, doing her crossword puzzle. When they separated—by twenty feet—she asked him to buy an extra Sunday *Times*, so she could solve the puzzle independently.

"You've rearranged the living room again," Albert says with a note of despair.

"Sean and Emily are coming home," Violet says. They have been in Fort Lauderdale, working in a car wash.

"Where will they sleep?"

"Here."

"Where will you sleep?"

"In a little nest I'm going to make in the living room, with white wicker furniture."

Albert tenderly pictures her curled in it at dawn, as in a birch grove, and is reminded of Turgenev.

"You can sleep in my room," he says magnanimously. Formerly this had been their room.

Violet shakes her head. Albert edges forward. Violet shrinks back, clutching the magazine section to her breast.

"I only wanted to see how far you'd got," he says.

"You only wanted to make fun of me," she says.

Albert decides to go through his ties. When he was younger, his mom was always after him to "go through" things, his dad to "get rid of them," his mom's concern being material—objects remorselessly overflow—his dad's spiritual: To be found in possession of dead flashlight batteries and headless lead grenadiers made one ineligible for the Kingdom of Heaven, or its sheolic equivalent.

Albert dumps the mass of ties on his bed. There are many more than he would have reckoned, and he has the fleeting notion they may have proliferated in the dark of his closet, like some kind of tropical growth. But when he examines them he realizes that, stained, narrow, somber for the most part, they represent more than twenty years of his life—in a sense, recapitulate it. That is, as, just casting his eyes over his bookshelves, he can almost recall with a greater wealth of detail where he read such and such a volume than its contents, so, surveying his ties, he can better remember the act of buying this or that one than the occasions upon which he wore it. In *this* sense, he reflects, I am a victim of circumstance. That is, substance eludes me.

Rummaging absently through the ties, as though tossing a great, gloomy salad, Albert thinks further: If I were to contemplate hanging myself by one of my neckties, how could I ever make up my mind which to knot about my throat? Also, if I wanted to make a less drastic escape by knotting my ties together and lowering myself out the window, how many stories' worth do I possess? In the literature, has anyone marked a significant correlation between the number of ties troubled urban souls own and the stories upon which they dwell? That is, do they usually have too few to reach the ground?

ALBERT imagines his apartment as it would look in one of those illustrations that used to appear at the beginning of mysteries: not a floor plan but a view from above and to one side, with the ceilings removed, so that the rooms and their furnishings—easy chairs in slipcovers, lamps with pleated shades, virtu—were revealed. The tenants never were shown, nor were there signs of habitation— the cushions would be perfectly plumped, the beds neatly made; no plants, no books, no pans of kitty litter. What this school of art had hit upon, Albert reflects, is that the way people live doesn't matter as much as their opportunities for entering and exiting unobserved.

This makes Albert recall a conversation he had with Violet earlier in the evening. He had gone into her room to say good night. She said that if the phone rang not to answer it (the extension was by his bed), as it would be for her. The phone was in the living room. To get to it, she would have to make two right turns: from the bedroom to the hall and from the hall to the living room. Albert said that to minimize the chances of his being awakened, he would now demonstrate how to reach the phone in the least number of rings. He lay down next to her on the bed. "It would be helpful," he said, "if you would sleep on your back on the extreme left side of the bed, with your feet more or less together. That way, when the first ring obtrudes into your subconscious you can swing your legs over the side and be fully erect in one fluid motion." He demonstrated. "Secondly, if you take the first turn a little wide, you'll be able to negotiate the second without decelerating. Please observe." She got out of bed to do so. "I'll now walk through it at half speed. You'll note that if I take the first turn too sharp, I have to pivot once, twice on my right foot, with a consequent loss of speed. I'd target for two rings, maximum."

"Don't forget to remember your dreams," Violet said. Dr. Nederlander had asked Albert to jot down his dreams.

"Don't give me the whole *farshtunkene* shooting script, Albert," he had said. "Just hit the highlights."

There is no relationship between the number of rooms portrayed in the frontispieces, Albert muses, and the number of bodies to be found sprawled in them. He pictures four recumbent figures on his premises: his, Violet's, Barney's, and Josh's. Presumably, Violet would be sleeping in her room, Barney in his, Josh on the living-room couch, barricaded behind throw cushions. This wasn't always the case. In the morning, when he went looking for Josh to walk him, Albert was frequently startled to find Violet in Barney's bed or Barney in Violet's when he gently lifted the covers. Recently, he discovered Josh in Violet's bed. For a moment, contemplating the grave, hoary muzzle, Albert thought he had found himself. On this occasion, Barney was in his bed and the couch was empty. Albert checked his own bed to see if Violet had slipped into it while he had been roaming about the apartment. It, too, was empty; she wasn't anywhere.

Albert ponders the baffling distribution of bodies. It seems to him less an instance of individuals switching beds behind his back than an illustration of the effects of propinquity. The members of his household were becoming interchangeable. It was as though they exchanged molecules; Albert imagines the tiny particles of matter jumping like fleas from one to the other.

Next he turns his attention to what his mom would call "articles of décor." In Barney's room, six gilded basketball players surmounting trophies eternally hold gilded basketballs aloft. In Violet's room, a cheap plastic elephant perpetually raises its trunk. In the living room, forsythia long since minus its blossoms arches over the couch, embowering Josh. The upward thrusts evince unspecified yearning. What if the sleepers simultaneously elevated their arms (and paws)?

"The first exercise tonight is the UNATTAINABLE REACHER," Albert announces from his bed. "It is a two-count exercise. In the starting position the body is supine, palms down. On the command ONE, swing arms vertically overhead, keeping the backs of the hands turned upward, fingers desperately clenching and unclenching. On the command TWO, return arms resignedly to the starting position, sighing in unison. In cadence, this exercise is performed as follows: (1) Starting position. (2) MOVE. In cadence, EXERCISE. One, two, *one*. One, two, *two*. One, two, *three* . . ."

LISTENING to the Milkman's Matinée on Barney's headset radio, Albert makes his way to the kitchen to get a tangerine. Opening the refrigerator he is dazzled by the burst of light, finding it comparable to the effulgence which in the Rembrandt print reveals the stirring Lazarus, floods Christ's robes. In that case, the light presumably emanates from the Lord instead of coming from behind the No-Cal cream soda, but the principle is the same. The Renaissance provides a wealth of examples of the Refrigerator Effect—a mysterious source of light, located below eye level in the middle ground.

Albert pulls out the vegetable bin. No tangies. He is on the point of letting the door shut on another inconsolable chapter of his life when the array of eggs catches his eye. Violet has written on them, "If you can't recall any dreams, you can have some of mine." Turning the eggs around, Albert gently inscribes them in ballpoint with his multitudinous dreams. He is relating how a basketball ref, about to present him with the ball to shoot a foul, instead whips out a revolver, when he runs out of eggs. Putting his clothes on over his pajamas, Albert heads for an all-night deli, meditating on *noctambulisme*, Baudelaire. The cashier is black, more nearly lustrously purple, *iridescent*, his cheeks adorned with tribal scars. He smirks as Albert puts three dozen jumbo on the counter, the scars silently opening and closing like fishes' mouths. Albert has the impression that he is participating in an instructive encounter—that the cashier belongs to one of those didactic tribes Wittgenstein kept invoking. Of course, he is also taking his master's at N.Y.U. Nowadays everyone is.

When Albert returns to bed and attempts to lay his head on the pillow, he fails to make contact. Investigating, he discovers he is still wearing the headset radio, and he feels his cheeks expanding in a savage smile.

WHEN the phone rings the first time, Albert beams, imagining Violet going through the drill, negotiating the corners with a slight body lean, arms gracefully flapping. Elapsed time: one abbreviated ring. The second phone call takes a ring and a half. Emboldened by her first, dazzling run, she must have pushed it too hard, lost control, and crashed into a wall. Albert compassionately speculates whether she sustained injuries. The third time the phone rings, Albert rips the receiver off and bellows, "I was almost asleep!"

"May I please speak to Violet?" Owen, the New Realist, whose token is the plastic elephant.

"You've overdone it, Owen," Albert says. "The cuckold, as comic hero, may be derided, but not reviled. *Three* phone calls isn't funny."

"The first two were from Emily," Violet says, picking up the phone in the living room. Is she holding her separated shoulder in place, Albert wonders.

"From Fort Lauderdale? What did she want?"

"She asked me to help her place the commas correctly in a long sentence."

"She's writing?"

"A postcard."

"And the second call?" Albert says, restriking the note of despair.

"To remind me to water her avocado. I didn't know you thought of yourself in heroic terms, Albert."

" 'The modern hero is no hero,' " Albert says. " 'He acts heroes. Heroic modernism turns out to be a tragedy in which the hero's part is available.' "

"That's not you, Albert," Violet says.

"Violet, 'As individuals express their life, so they are.' "

"That's not you, either."

"Nope, Marx."

"And the other?"

"Walter Benjamin."

"Don't know him, old boy," Owen says.

"You stay out of this, Owen," Albert says.

"Are you insinuating that you're up for the part, Albert?" Violet asks.

"My dime's running out," Owen mutters.

" '*Je suivais, roidissant mes nerfs comme un héros,*' " Albert chants.

"Albert, it's late," Violet says. "Hang up your end."

" '*Et discutant avec mon âme déjà lasse . . .*' " he murmurs before breaking off. "I'm a roomer in my own house."

"It's what you always wanted from us," Violet says. "It gives you so many opportunities for remoteness."

RETURNING to the kitchen, Albert reflects that for the first time in his life he has been nearly guilty of aposiopesis. He'd have to remember to tell Dr. Nederlander. Opening the refrigerator, he kneels before the devotional light. He is admiring how the Saran Wrap covering a dish of left-over bass formidably shimmers like the raiments in the Rembrandt painting of one-eyed Julius Civilis, when the phone rings. As he goes to answer it, he dimly makes out Violet, diligently barrelling through the switches. Her arms *are* flapping, and as she hits the straight and accelerates he is put in mind of a great wading bird lifting off at dawn, as in a portentous dream.

"I've got it," Albert says the moment before they collide.

"I hope I'm not disturbing you."

"My dad," Albert says, holding the receiver against his chest with one hand, helping Violet to her feet with the other, drawing her to him so she can listen in.

"No, Dad, I wasn't asleep."

"I wasn't, either. I couldn't finish the puzzle. It kept preying on my mind. When you get old, words elude you. What's 30 down, for God's sake?"

Philodemos said thought would console you when you can no longer enjoy the act of love, Albert reflects, but he didn't mention words slipping away, being haunted by unfilled spaces. Fall warblers come to mind, remotely flitting, undifferentiated, his eyes spectrally tearing, recalling spring.

Violet brings him *his* magazine section. As he gives his dad the answers, his dad swears, groans, chuckles in his ear, lulling and melodious as doves. He will have to tell Dr. Nederlander about this obsessive bird metaphorizing as well. Albert lies down where Violet intends to make her nest, remembering how his dad would come into his room and sing him to sleep. Violet stretches out alongside, finding the places in the puzzle for him. Like Turgenev, looking up Albert gazes into a bottomless sea.

SIX

THE BEDROOM FLOOR creaks alarmingly when Albert does his push-ups. What if it gave way and he descended, outstretched, into the apartment below like a poorly coordinated quattrocento angel? Suppose he crashed through a number of apartments in a hail of lath, plaster, Sheetrock, excelsior, whatever's in there, his undershorts fluttering, wearing what an astonished succession of tenants took to be an insipid smile but was in fact an artistic convention.

This, he realizes, is preposterous; he lives on the third floor. Plummeting through *two* apartments to fetch up in a boiler room wouldn't be worth the pain and suffering, regardless of the sensation he caused. Worse, there might be nobody at home. To drop unnoticed through vacant rooms seems to Albert to be an act that could only lower one's spirits. He imagines such a melancholy descent, past shuddering rhododendron that had seen better days and bunched upholstery from which appalled cats shot up.

Then the idea came to him: What if one found oneself falling through one's former apartments, the earliest bottommost, as though they were embedded in geological strata? He might flash by Violet, his semi-ex-wife, and Barney and Emily doing a jigsaw puzzle of "The Death of Sardanapalus" in a newly renov 3 BR w/wbf, A/C, brk walls, and 24-hr secu, imploring their forgiveness, signifying his inadvertence, regret, dismay, whatever, and gathering, amid a blizzard of fragmented slaves and concubines, that they had interpreted his wild gestures as an unsuccessful attempt to execute a forward two-and-a-half with a twist or similar dive with a high degree of difficulty. Mindful that Schopenhauer said you could no more express two thoughts at the same time than think them, he will strive for intelligibility in the charming duplex overlooking gdns w/clsts galore, but plunging into a darkened bedroom he makes out Violet, her face smoother, her trust intact, sleeping on her side, the fingers of her left hand clasping those of the man who lies next to her, his arm thrust between her thighs, and who Albert assumes is himself. (This arrangement of limbs is conjectural; a sheet nearly covers them. As though restoring his own ruined work, Albert fearfully extends and entwines.)

The phone rings, and he is left hanging in air.

"Albert, you're a patsy."

It's his dad, the attorney-at-law, *in re* the separation agreement. Albert pictures him in his office, light flashing off framed citations from charitable organizations, holding his ancient, heavy handset with one hand, a pencil poised in the other, in case he has to make "notations." These he always "jots down" on irregular scraps of paper he produces from a mysterious supply.

"You have an overgenerous nature," his dad goes on. "You're throwing away your future. You're depriving me of negotiating room."

Once again Albert has the impression that it is his dad and Violet who are separating, and that his vain function is to mediate their differences.

"I'm getting together with her attorney," his dad is saying, "but if that young whippersnapper thinks I'm going to traipse all the way down to lower Broadway, he . . . I know the building. No one has offices there anymore."

Albert summons up a dim lobby with cracked marble facing, his dad scrutinizing the directory as though it were a corrupt text.

"Albert, why are you breathing so hard?" It's his mom, on the extension. In fact, his dad is at home.

"I was in the midst of my push-ups."

"Don't overtax yourself in this difficult period. If you're having dinner with us tomorrow, come before six. That way you and Dad can listen to the news together."

Albert falls through brite, lux 1½s in which he had hummed more frequently than he realized—in one sep kit a naked woman on the verge of tears, whom he can't place, is patting bacon with a paper towel—before crashing into a series of spacious 7 rms w/hi ceils and w/w cptg where his parents, ever younger, are listening to the news. How do they react to their son's barging in on them this way? In the first apartment, his mom begs Albert to shield his eyes if he intends to keep this up, as they are his most precious asset; his dad irritably turns up the volume; a comic maid drops a tray and says "Lawdy!" In the second apartment, his mom tells Albert he ought to treat himself to some decent underwear, since he will undoubtedly come under the scrutiny of strangers; his dad makes a face in response to her suggestion, but it is unclear what has displeased him, form or content; a different comic maid drops a tray and says "Lawdy!" In the third apartment, his parents stare blankly at the intruder. They have failed to associate the grieving, dishevelled middle-aged man with the child in the next room; so, Albert painfully concludes, has he.

"As WE periodically fall, demanding explanations from the past, like great clouds of gnats, words irresistibly rise from the pages where they had so restlessly teemed," Albert informs Violet after tracking her down in the International. Pushing her cart through the narrow aisles, he marks how the supermarket resembles a catacomb. He goes on, talking to her back as she hefts cantaloupes like skulls: "They get in our ears, our eyes, our noses, maddening us; we submit to their high, insistent buzzing—"

"Gnats are inarticulate, Albert," Violet says, holding a cantaloupe to her ear, thumping it, listening for the resonant note of ripeness, which he has never been able to distinguish.

Albert says, "Furthermore, in the next to last apartment I caught a glimpse of myself. I was four."

She shoves the cantaloupe under his nose. "Now breathe deeply, Albert."

"You know the porcelain heron on the lamp in the living room? I was stroking its feathers, as though I could warm it to life."

"It won't work," she says. "I tried it on you for eleven years. Can you smell it, Albert?"

"No. And don't make me squeeze any pears." He is unreasonably bereft. "I can't tell the difference."

"Oh, Albert. 'By what we do we know what we are, just as by what we suffer we know what we deserve.' "

"Who said that?"

"Buzz, buzz. Schopenhauer."

Now, *aetat.* forty-five, Albert stands in the shower energetically shaking a bottle of shampoo under the mistaken impression it is Italian dressing. It has just struck him that Violet and he have not discussed who is going to get the Instamatic. This came to him during his precipitate tour of the past, for Violet and he are still imprisoned upside down in the back of the camera, a roll started at Wellfleet the summer before not having been finished. Albert recalls posing for the last shot. "Stick your nose in my ear," he has whispered. Violet has a long, shapely nose, like the Comtesse de Noailles. "I'm not putting it in there anymore," she had hissed back. So they were condemned to hang from their heels apart—not, admittedly, for eternity, but until the emulsion deteriorated.

This puts Albert in mind of the fact that in ancient libraries books were chained to desks. He imagines them straining to get loose, snapping in Latin. Or a group of restless scholars, books in hand, pacing around a desk, punctiliously raising or lowering their chains to allow a colleague to pass under or step over; or, lost in thought, neglecting this courtesy, so that they become bound together in a great ball; or one absently wandering to the end of his tether and being jerked off his feet, as if emphasizing that knowledge has its limits.

Parallels may be drawn with the state of marriage, Albert reflects, brushing his teeth. Before he and Violet separated, he kept his toothbrushes on the right side of the fixture; hers were on the left, and thus they lay in bed. Now Albert realizes he is so habituated to living in half the available space that he has preserved this arrangement; if she were unexpectedly to rejoin him, the accustomed holes would be free to receive her toothbrushes, and she could slip between the sheets in the dark without asking him to shove over.

So, in fact, she often had come to bed in the last days of their marriage. If she wasn't home when Albert was ready to turn out the light, he would start calling the three bars she frequented. When she came to the phone, he would say, "When do you want me to set the alarm?"

If his dad knew that this sort of thing had gone on, it would only confirm his opinion that Violet had let him down, and he would say to Albert, "You've effectively tied my hands on the alimony by mentioning a figure when I asked you to refrain from making any offers, but I'm not going to let you fork over a lump sum up front."

"I just want to do what's fair," Albert would say.

"Fair, fair, you've been fair. Now you're being guilty. What have you to feel guilty about? Who started it?"

"I told you—it was virtually simultaneous."

Albert imagines this conversation while watching his dad squeeze lemon into his tea as though he were wringing out a bathing suit, and he realizes that a disproportionate amount of his childhood was devoted to wringing out bathing suits under his dad's supervision.

"Do you want more coffee, Albert?" his mom asks.

"No."

"Just half a cup?"

"Do you know what the hardest things to get in

America are?" Albert says. "A half a cup of coffee and an AM radio you can plug in. I went to a place on Fourteenth Street and said, 'I would like to buy an AM radio you can plug in. No portable, no FM, no police band, no ship-to-shore.' The clerk said, 'I have a very nice radio for thirteen dollars.' I said, 'But that one has a clock. I have a clock. I want a radio without a clock.' The clerk said, 'I'll let you have it for twelve.' I said, 'You're not following me. I want the radio for my bedside table, upon which there is already a clock. What am I supposed to do with two clocks? I want a little, plastic AM radio you don't have to buy batteries for so I can listen to the news. I was raised to listen to the news twice a day. What's happened to those little radios? Where did they all go?' The clerk said, 'It's yours for nine-fifty. Think of it this way: a clock would set you back five, so you're getting the radio for four and a half bucks.' Insofar as a half of cup of coffee is concerned, I defy you to show me a restaurant where you wind up with less than two-thirds of a cup. Three-quarters is the rule."

"I hope you didn't let her have your clock, Albert," his mom says.

"Your mother got that clock for you by depositing five hundred dollars in a savings account," his dad says.

"She has the clock," his mom tells his father.

When Albert is getting his coat from the closet, his mom says, "Why don't you try on Uncle Arthur's overcoats?"

Uncle Arthur had died the month before, at the age of eighty-five. His three black coats hang next to Albert's, revealing nothing, as Schopenhauer noted about overcoats and men, of the man who wore them.

"Is this a new tactic in your campaign to disparage my pile-lined coat?" Albert says.

"Dad says they're too voluminous for him," his mom says.

Albert fingers a sleeve.

"One hundred percent cashmere," his mom says. "Uncle Arthur liked quality."

"He ate in the best restaurants," his dad says.

"In his overcoat?" Albert says.

"Maître d's greeted him by name," his mom says. "We had them cleaned, of course."

"What am I going to do with *three* overcoats?" Albert says.

"You can rotate them," his mom says.

"Allow me," his dad says, holding one so Albert can slip it on.

The second is bigger than the first, the third bigger still, as though for some mysterious purpose Uncle Arthur had them made so they could be worn one on top of the other. Albert goes through the pockets in case Uncle Albert left an explanatory note.

When he gets home, Albert hangs the coats in his hall closet; they suggest the presence of three natty strangers of slightly differing size in his living room. Perhaps, hearing that he was plagued with uncertainty, Brown, Jones, and Robinson, the three faceless men who hire themselves out to philosophers for demonstrations (Smith and the King of France are other members of the firm), have arrayed themselves on his couch, their well-scrubbed hands resting on their knees.

Albert sits on the side of the bed, vaults obliquely into

it, and by a series of dexterous movements contrives to wrap himself in the covers—a system perfected by Kant. But he cannot sleep because of the intense cold; Violet has the comforter pending the final agreement. *Les pardessus de mon oncle!* Albert lays the coats, which had been an ornament to so many restaurant checkrooms, on top of the blankets and springs back into bed.

The sleeves of the bottommost coat lightly embrace him. "Albert, I want to clear up this coat business for you," Uncle Arthur says. "One's not bigger than the next; what they are is smaller. As you grow older, Albert, you shrink. Take Kant, a great man. He boasted how he'd triumphantly maintained his balance on the slack rope of life for almost eighty years. In the end he was a midget like everybody else. What can I tell you, Albert? I hope you live long enough to see the Cuban embargo lifted so you can get a nice cigar to smoke. Another thing: never overlook the captain; it's not *au fait*. Slip a nicely folded bill into his palm. And don't be *too* surreptitious. You're not sneaking him a state secret, you're dining out."

This aspect of spying arises again the following morning. Albert and Violet arrange by phone to leave their apartments—they live three blocks apart—at nine-thirty on the dot and meet on Sixth Avenue, Violet to hand over Albert's mail, Albert to hand over Violet's Chinese laundry, which he will have picked up en route. "J 954, green," she says, speaking through a handkerchief to disguise her voice.

When the exchange has taken place, Albert says, "Violet, when are you going to let me come over and get some more of my books?"

"Albert, I told you that leaves holes."

"Holes, holes. You think I don't have any holes in my house? My whole life's full of holes."

"You're not preying on the weakness of women anymore?"

"Actually, Violet, I'm feeding on my own."

"Oh, Albert, you'll utterly consume yourself. There'll be nothing left."

"No, the reverse. I've finally figured out what's going to happen to me."

"Which is?"

"I'm going to become more of what I am. I'll make a deal with you, Violet. If you let me have two shopping bags full of books I'll put new bulbs in your ceiling fixtures for you. No, you like living in the dark. If Kant lived in the dark, you can live in the dark. Do you want me to string up a rope to help you find the can, or wherever it was he went, hand over hand, as though nightly condemned to scale the same terrible peak, pondering the interaction between the things he bumped into and himself?"

ALBERT takes the train to Connecticut to see his twenty-eight-year-old girl friend, the Human Dynamo. She finishes telling him off in her driveway. "You don't play tennis, you don't snow-ski, you don't water-ski, you don't ride a bicycle, you're the last one off the train, you *plod* across the parking lot. Albert, we have nothing in common."

"I seem to have little in common with anyone," he says, failing to heave himself out of her BMW on the first try.

He stands beneath the pines in front of the converted

pool house she is renting. Before she turns off the head-lights, he sees it is beginning to snow.

"And you huff and puff when you make love," she says, taking his arm. "You should see your face."

"What would I see?"

"Strain," says the Human Dynamo. "Anguish. Despair."

As she lets him in, it strikes Albert that if they stopped seeing each other he'd be stuck with an odd number of eggs. Three weeks ago, when he moved into his own place, she stayed over and had an egg for breakfast. As Albert always has two, there has been an odd number in his refrigerator ever since. Albert foresees this haunting disparity continuing indefinitely; an old man, he opens the refrigerator and sighs, knowing that yet again he will be confronted with five eggs or eleven. On the other hand, he reflects that if he hadn't got separated he never would have known how much he valued symmetry.

"The special tonight is spaghetti," the Human Dynamo announces, setting a pot of water on the stove.

Albert is sitting at the kitchen table in one of Uncle Arthur's overcoats, listening to the news and snipping frost-blackened leaves off a miserable avocado plant. The Human Dynamo keeps her thermostat at fifty-five—the lowest possible setting—to stimulate the circulation; her house is full of stunted or vestigial plants. Albert breathes through his mouth—a practice Kant considered insalu-brious—to find out if he can see his breath. It plumes from his mouth like a comic-strip balloon in which noth-ing is written.

"If you're all that cold, stand by the stove," she says.

He joins her next to the steaming pot. They are en-veloped in a column of romantic vapor. Slipping his hands beneath the Human Dynamo's turtleneck, Albert listens to the boiling spaghetti. The sound is of a dozen pens industriously scratching, and he feels his life has become a mockery.

ALBERT does not believe in causality. Nor does he have any truck with destiny, chance, or sortilege. However, he dabbles in numerology to the extent that he has an "operative number"; this is the term he uses to distinguish it from a lucky number, inasmuch as he does not invoke it for divine audition or to solicit good fortune, but to carry out a pattern. Three, ten, and one hundred are common examples of what might be called operative numbers. We often perform acts in threes or on three, or count to ten or one hundred before taking, or abandoning, action.

Albert's number is thirty-two. In the morning, he counts silently to thirty-two before getting out of bed— or to sixty-four or to ninety-six; in certain situations multiples are admissible. (Albert weighed one hundred and ninety-two pounds until recently, when he went on a diet. Alas, one-sixty is beyond reach.) Going to work, he chooses the subway exit where thirty-two steps lead to the surface; these he ascends with uncharacteristic jauntiness. At his desk he downs his cup of coffee in thirty-two rapid, intense sips. Before retiring, he does thirty-two sit-ups, thirty-two push-ups, reads thirty-two pages, and turns out the light.

Now, making love to the Human Dynamo, Albert executes one hundred and twenty-eight strokes.

"I can see you moving your lips," she says midway.

Albert awakens early and sits up in bed. Chin in hand, he

contemplates the Human Dynamo, whose back protrudes from the disordered covers like the ivory hilt of an ornamental dagger that had been thrust at him in the night and missed. So had Sardanapalus surveyed the tumult and wreckage of his life.

Albert goes to the window; it is still snowing. The pool house is built on a rise; a narrow brook emptying into a pond runs at the bottom of the lawn. These are now frozen. Movement in the second growth on the far side of the brook catches his eye. At first he thinks a little old man is emerging from the wood, carrying each foot to the ground and setting it firmly down, the way Kant got around in his last years. When the man gets clear of the trees, Albert realizes that he is in fact an upright and prodigious bird, a great blue heron stalking through the mottling snow. Albert regards its resplendent, metrical approach. As Japanese screens are meant to be viewed while one is seated on the floor and lose something when seen from a standing position, so Albert fears he is too high up to appreciate what is unfolding and rushes downstairs to the kitchen. However, when he gets to the kitchen window, the bird is gone, its tracks filled in with snow.

"Kant was a bird watcher," the Human Dynamo says when Albert returns to the bedroom. She is standing naked by the window, looking out. "He could distinguish them by their songs. You never sing, Albert," she adds, getting back in bed. "How can you expect anyone to know who you are?"

"I'M being painted," Albert tells Violet on the phone. "I thought you said it didn't need painting."

"I was mistaken. Peach depresses me. So do hundreds of little ducks."

"What are you talking about, Albert?"

"The wallpaper. They waddle from right to left. It's perverse."

"I don't follow you."

"Like words, life flows from left to right. You open a book with your left hand, you close it with your right. Commuter trains arrive from the left and depart to the right, except at Jamaica, Croton-Harmon, and 125th Street. When men kiss women's breasts, they invariably elect to kiss the nipple to their left first. In the morning you put on the left sock before the right and at night you take them off in the same order. Consider their shape and you will agree that too often they serve as parentheses—which, by the way, Schopenhauer deplored—enclosing yet another day's digression."

"All very well, Albert, but why did you call?"

"To ask whether you'd let me stay with you when they do my bedroom."

"If you bring your pillows."

Several nights later, Albert, wrapped in another of Uncle Arthur's overcoats, plods up Sixth Avenue, a pillow under each arm. This, he thinks, is how I'd have carried my children, if I had had any. When I married Violet her kids were too big to tuck under the arm and break into a run. Emotions have a left–right flow, too, but rarely preserve their character en route, wishes forming at the left and straggling off as disappointments at the right.

SEVEN

THE HUMAN DYNAMO SAYS, "Are Jewish people always sad when they pack?" She is lounging on Albert's bed, watching a World Team Tennis match on television without the sound, which Albert won't let her turn up because life is hard enough—admittedly, he has told her, a state of affairs he doesn't expect her to recognize at twenty-eight. Off to Miami in the morning, he is traipsing back and forth between his dresser and his suitcase, carrying a shirt or a little pile of underwear, as though they were relics he was bearing in a religious procession. "You're slowing down," the Human Dynamo says. "You misjudged the pace."

Albert inwardly concurs. He has rated his life incorrectly; he is forty-five, the finish line is within sight, and there is too much ground to make up.

"I'm going to rephrase my question," the Human Dynamo announces. "Are all Jewish people sad when they pack?"

Balling a pair of socks, Albert decides he's not so much sad as disquieted and wonders why. All that comes to mind is that the pool will be full of shrieking children or drained for repairs and he won't be able to go swimming. Albert is haunted by the spectre of empty pools; they figure in his dreams—immense, freshly dug graves. This, he realizes, is an anxiety unlikely to afflict many of his fellow-men, and thus sets him dubiously apart.

"I'm going to descend from the general to the particular," the Human Dynamo says. "Did you ask Violet to console you while you packed?"

ONE night a week later, back from his trip, Albert stares out of his bedroom window. This overlooks a yard in which he once saw an ovenbird circumspectly walking beneath a rank rose of Sharon bush, so that for a moment he had the unsettling impression he was deep in the country rather than on the third and top floor of a Federal house in the Village. Before he and Violet split up six months ago, they rented the apartment in the elevator building two blocks away, which I have described; she has continued to live there with Barney, Emily, and Josh. From his bedroom, Albert can see a corner of Violet's building, if not the windows of her apartment. If he could look in, Albert fancies he would behold events that happened far in the past, as though the brightly lit windows were heavenly bodies, and learn whatever lessons history teaches.

"Oh, God," his mom had said when Albert told her where he had moved. "You can hear her hair dryer from there. Couldn't you have put more ground between your-selves?'"

"It wasn't premeditated," Albert said. "It was a super-venient turn of events. If you visualize the marriage as a ship that has broken up, you will see us as two shipmates clinging to opposite ends of a large piece of flotsam."

"I see you as two idiots awash on a delusion," his dad said.

"Be that as it may," Albert said, "it also means I can walk Josh now and then." Under the terms of the separa-tion agreement, Violet got Josh, so he wouldn't have to climb stairs; Albert got the Boston fern.

BEFORE he gets into bed to read, Albert goes into the little bedroom giving off his and transfers the fern from the windowsill to a pedestal table. This way, when he looks up from his book he can see the fern and its reflec-tion; he has hung a mirror behind the table for just this purpose. Besides augmenting the green, reposeful rise and fall of the fronds, which, when faintly agitated by a draft, enhance the illusion that the plant is a fountain, the mirror extends his vista since it appears to afford a view of an empty room beyond it rather than reflecting the one in which he lies unseen. All that is visible in the mirror is an oblong of white wall. If it were not for the venous hands holding the book, Albert thinks, he would be merely a pair of incorporeal eyes by means of which words evenly flowed, maintaining their spacing, to an immaterial brain. Albert reflects that he is doing little more than placing himself in the way of the endless stream of words, which by and large pass through him like cosmic rays.

Albert's gaze is drawn to his fern; this, luxuriant, sits

on the pedestal table like a green Persian cat. How much we have in common, he muses: silence, self-containment, seeming contemplativeness. Man may be a thinking reed, Albert acknowledges, but he wonders whether others have as appallingly few thoughts as he does—not vagrant notions or impressions but carefully mediated achievement. Violet used to accuse him of secrecy, of mocking her, when she asked him what he was thinking and he said "Nothing." But this was nearly the case.

Albert has a sudden, sentimental urge to take the fern in his arms. Every morning, in fact, he does so, picking it up like a cat, or a baby, or perhaps a human head, and carrying it into the bathroom to get the benefit of the humidity when he takes his shower. Anyone who hasn't lifted a cat or a baby for a while will find them surprisingly heavy; the same perhaps holds for a human head. If, of course, you could just carry the fern itself, it would be as nothing, as weightless as the thoughts of a lifetime; it's the burden of the compacted earth that astonishes.

A sudden, obscure, conceivably oracular utterance startles Albert, for three reasons: first, although it is apparently in English, he can't grasp what was said; second, he doesn't know who said it; lastly, he doesn't know where the speaker is. This is the order of his concern. Albert doubts whether someone else in his position would have established the same hierarchy. It is probably things like this that set him apart from his fellow-men, he decides.

At any rate, he eventually finds by his side another man's wife, whose presence he has forgotten, muttering in her sleep. He slips a hand under her head and hefts it.

"What are you up to now, Albert?" she says.

"I'm weighing your head."

"What do you think—is it a keeper?"

Albert glances at his alarm clock. "Will you excuse me?" he says, getting out of bed. "I've got to intercept Mills."

Every night at eleven, Albert's landlord, Mills, who with his family occupies the parlor and second floors, leaves the house to jog through the streets of New York, returning at midnight.

Standing on the sidewalk in his raincoat, pajamas, and slippers, as if he has been evacuated because of a fire or gas leak, Albert peers toward Fifth Avenue, waiting for Mills to materialize. In a few minutes he comes into view, pounding down the middle of the street in his burnt-orange sweatsuit with the white competition stripes. When he passes in front of his house, he arches his chest and throws up his arms, as though breasting a tape or invoking a greater authority.

"Mills, a word," Albert says, stepping off the curb.

"Gotta warm down," Mills gasps, swivelling his head, shaking out his arms, capering toward Sixth.

Albert trots alongside. "It's about the bulbs, Mills."

"Bulbs?" Mills pants.

"They're out again. Three of the five in the chandelier in the vestibule that are supposed to resemble little flames, the one in the entranceway, and one of the two flanking the front door that are stipulated by the Housing Maintenance Code. Mills, I realize we belong to two extreme schools of thought respecting dead bulbs, neither of which perhaps is socially desirable. You are indifferent to them almost to a perverse degree. I, on the other hand, am traumatized by dead bulbs—particularly in ceiling fixtures. My gaze is fatally drawn upward in the manner of cinquecento saints whenever I pass beneath them. Wait a minute—I lost a slipper."

Having reached the corner, Mills turns and jogs back to where Albert is forlornly hopping about and offers him his shoulder so he can put on the slipper without stepping on the pavement with his bare foot, which would mortify his mom. Albert's mind retains the impress of such things.

"I'm going to take care of the bulbs right away," Mills says.

"You've made these promises before," Albert says. They are climbing the stoop. Submissively noting the dark coach lamp, Albert forces his gaze higher. Wisteria, in whose thick coils innumerable sparrows presumably sleep, engulfs the façade, as though, Albert muses, centuries had passed since he got out of bed and the building had fallen into picturesque decay. "No one forced you to convert it into a multiple dwelling," he tells Mills.

"I didn't know you subscribed to free will, Albert," Mills says.

ALBERT hangs up his raincoat and climbs back into bed, brushing against a bulky object he can't place. Withdrawing to the edge of the bed, he considers this encounter. Given that my life is a demonstration of Hume's discontinuous present, he thinks, what we have here might equally be a prie-dieu, an incomplete set of *Notable British Trials*, or my dad. Albert reaches out: she has slipped his mind for the second time.

"Would you accommodate a fantasy of mine?" she says.

"Just my métier," Albert says sadly. "What would you

like me to be, a weak-hitting third baseman or a poet *manqué*?"

In a few moments, the phone rings.

"I just wanted to let you know there's nothing in this house to read."

"Who am I speaking to?" Albert says.

"You're speaking to Violet, who's been through two marriages, and both times all the books have gone. Here I am, a fairly literate person, and all I've got on my bookshelves is junk."

"But you got the jelly cupboard and the Gabon funerary figure and the seashells."

"And you got the apothecary jars and the ashtray from the Colony and the pie cupboard *and* all the Elizabeth Bowens."

THE next morning, Albert walks down Sixth Avenue, carrying a dead iris that hadn't fully opened. He goes into Mother Nature's Creative Gardens, where he buys his flowers.

"Has Mother let you down again, Albert?" Donald, the proprietor, asks, addressing him from between two great lilac branches, which he has parted.

"It never unfurled, Donald."

"Didn't say 'Ah'—is that what you're telling me, Albert?" Donald says, scrutinizing the shrivelled petals. "Did I ever tell you you're the only customer I have who returns flowers?"

"It seems to be a recurring theme," Albert says. "I recently returned a loaf of raisin bread to Jefferson Market—"

"What was wrong with it?"

"No raisins. They told me it was a first. Donald, I sometimes think it's things like this that set me apart from my
fellow-men. Are you going to give me a refund or another
flower?"

"What did Jefferson give you?"

"Another loaf. There weren't any raisins in that one,
either."

"I think you've been singled out by Providence, Albert."

"These lilacs any good?"

"Please don't shake them, Albert. You shake quince,
you shake dogwood, you don't shake lilacs. They're too
big for you anyway. They'll tip your pot over."

"I can manage."

"Albert, listen to me. You're not going to be able to
handle them. I happen to know that these lilacs are beyond
your capability. They're going to get the upper hand.
You want me to pick up the *Post* and read 'MAN WRESTLES
GIANT LILACS, LOSES'?"

"Albert, they're out of the question."

It's his mom, advancing, withdrawing an iris from a
vase to see if its stem is split.

"Are you coming from your knee therapy at St.
Vincent's or your body-language class at the New
School?" Albert asks.

She turns to Donald. "My son has a poor grasp of
reality," she says in a confidential tone. "He overextends
his bounds."

"Only in little things," Albert says. "Insofar as great
issues are concerned, I know my place."

"Are you coming to dinner?" his mom says. "I'm making Tou Goo Gai Kew."

"My mom has taken up Chinese cooking," Albert tells
Donald.

"I've *taken* Chinese cooking," his mom says. "Now I'm taking *advanced* Chinese cooking." Albert wonders what lies in store for him at seventy-five. Lately he has the feeling that he is not so much pursuing his destiny as furiously racing alongside it, the way cars race trains in old movies.

AFTER dinner, Albert settles into his dad's chair at one end of the living room; his mom and dad draw up bridge chairs. While his mom tells him she is thinking of having his comforter restuffed, Albert looks past her at the bookcase at the other end of the room, where a large photograph of him and Violet embracing beneath the pines in Wellfleet is propped, and discovers he has his arms around Shakespeare. A *Hamlet* paperback has been placed to obliterate Violet, the Droeshout portrait on the cover coinciding with her hidden face.

"While I'm at it," his mom is saying, "I'm going to have it recovered, but definitely not in satin."

"What's wrong with satin?" his dad asks.

"Satin is slithery. Don't you find it slithers off, Albert?"

"Slides," says his dad, compulsively hitching a trouser leg. " 'Slithers' implies volition."

"Your dad is always squelching me, but he can't snuff out my artistic flame. Don't you find it slips off, Albert?"

"I don't mind," says Albert, regarding Shakespeare and himself—Shakespeare somewhat quizzical, as though having second thoughts about their collaboration, he with a lunatic grin. "It gives me something to do in the middle of the night."

"Whatever do you mean?" his mom asks.

"Groping for the comforter. It's almost as though it's some vast, rudimentary invertebrate, which, no matter how assiduously trained, instinctively seeks its natural habitat on the floor when its master is asleep."

"Cotton," his mom pronounces, biting into an after-dinner mint.

"What about cotton?" his dad says.

"Cotton will put an end to all that."

"The way you've so neatly put an end to Violet?" Albert says, gesturing toward the bookshelf.

"Why should she be on display here?" his mom says. "She's not a part of our lives."

Albert reflects that nowadays he is barely part of his own life. It undeviatingly extends without seeming to require his presence. He plays a minor role, if any, like that of a page turner at a recital.

Not so much quizzical, Albert decides, reappraising Shakespeare, as speculative, as though Shakespeare were considering the disrepair of his own life; of course, it's hard to tell with gentiles. Or perhaps he was only listening to a pine warbler. High above, one was periodically singing, Albert recalls, rending their hearts, when the shutter fell.

ALBERT and the Human Dynamo take the noon balloon to Boston to see the sixth game of the World Series. In the Ritz, she says, "Which do you think is bigger, your whizzer or a World Series ticket?"

"I'd say it's a tossup," he says.

"I'd say you have delusions of grandeur."

"If I have any delusions," Albert says, "they are ones of insignificance."

"Not from there," the Human Dynamo says. "Come on, you've got to play fair."

"So my father has told me. Last night, while we were having Tou Goo Gai Kew, he said, 'You're fondling your silverware again. If you fondle it here where mother and I can overlook it or forgive you because you're our son, you'll fondle it when you're dining out where it will reflect falsely on your rearing.' "

"Let's face it, Albert, you just don't measure up."

"It wasn't a fair test. I digressed."

ALBERT and the Human Dynamo fly to L.A., rent a car, and drive into the dun hills above El Toro, where she will go to tennis camp while he reads *Historia Animalium* by the pool.

One afternoon she suddenly looms above his chaise in her tennis clothes, furiously weeping. He closes Aristotle on a finger and motions her to one side, because she is blocking his sun. "I thought the 'B's were doing the overhead between three and five," he says.

She glares at him, then stalks off toward the road that winds higher into the hills. He follows her progress. Now and then, she is hidden from view; each time she reappears, she is more remote, smaller. It is his wish that she should vanish altogether. What business has he seeing someone so young?

When she has been out of sight an hour, he goes to their unit. Opening the door, he hears her tearfully chanting, " 'Point with relaxed arm, chin up, hit ball in front of body, hit up and through ball, snap wrist . . .' " She is standing naked by the kitchenette counter, practicing overheads, and he is charmed anew.

"Don't cry," he says. "You're a darling girl."

"But I can't do overheads," she wails.

"Surely that's nothing to cry about."

"Don't Jewish people ever cry?"

"At the movies," he says, recalling that Violet used to accuse him of being afraid to succumb to his emotions except in the Greenwich or the Waverly.

By and by, they get on the bed. Lying sideways toward the end, Albert considers Aristotle's boar, which, in its declining years, "finding itself unable to accomplish the sexual commerce with due speed, and growing fatigued with the standing posture, will roll the sow over on the ground, and the pair will conclude the operation side by side of one another."

And, Albert concedes, at literary allusions as well.

THE next week, Albert runs into Violet on his way to the laundromat and tells her about the comforter.

"I'll say one thing about that old puff," she says. "I spent many a night of our marriage sewing the panels where they were ripped. Like the Turks plastering over St. Sophia, your mother's striving to efface every last vestige of my artistry."

"I never saw you sewing it up."

"I did it when you were off on your trips, unable to sleep for fear the pool would be full of kids or that they were about to let the water out. Then, as now, you never spared a thought for me or your stepchildren."

"I did. I do. Yesterday, I brought each of you a bottle of multi-vitamins with minerals."

"Don't worry. We're not going to contribute to your load of moral accountability by dropping dead of scurvy. What have you got in that shopping bag—one of your perpetually ailing plants?"

"My laundry. But since you mention it, mushrooms are growing in my philodendrons."

"It's probably a consequence of the lugubrious atmosphere in which you live. Milton says you always look as if you're going to cry."

"Who's Milton?"

"He folds at the laundromat to put himself through N.Y.U. nights."

Albert finds Milton folding primrose facecloths in the back of the laundromat. "This here's a vast, untapped mine of the human comedy," he says, indicating the ranks of throbbing washers. "If you want to look into the heart of man, look at his laundry. A case in point. This particular customer's load invariably contains two bath towels—one his, one his old lady's. No hand towels, no facecloths; they don't use them. However, in this bundle spread out before me what do we find but *three* bath towels, *two* hand towels, *two* facecloths. Now, from long acquaintance with the customer's laundry, I know he's a reasonably fastidious dude, but for a while back what do we get for two weeks running but *one* bath towel minus the few feminine garments that aren't of delicate fabric construction that are customarily in the bundle. For the last couple of weeks, I'm folding the stuff you see before you minus the feminine garments per the previous two weeks.

"Now I'm going to give you the fruits of my protracted labors in the human vineyard. Since they dried themselves with individual bath towels, the *one* bath towel two weeks running indicates to me his old lady cut out on him. If it was for only a week, she's ten–twelve to be in Jersey, visiting her mother. For two weeks he's a lost soul, going

· *101* ·

to Jefferson to buy a nice piece of haddock for dinner, watching a little Channel 13, take half a Valium, and so to bed. Time passes, and in accordance with the great cycle of nature, life begins anew. He starts calling up chicks from days of yore. To make a long story short: *three* bath towels, *two* hand towels, *two* facecloths."

"And me and Violet?"

"A painful case. I can't help recollecting how you used to lug in those big five-dollar, six-dollar loads. Now the two of you show up with these dainty little bundles. Albert, after folding someone's stuff week after week you get a certain rapport going with the garments, a very warm, personal feeling. Those items originally came in here together, Albert, and they belong together. Whenever it's humanly possible, I throw yours and Violet's in the same machine. It gives me good vibes to see them being agitated en masse in the wash cycle, tumbling amongst one another in the dryer's warm embrace."

Albert finds himself looking into one of the dryers. Behind the glass door, clothes appear and reappear, seemingly striving with death-defying leaps to reach an unattainable objective: to be something more exalted than garments, Albert guesses. He recalls the long hairs, so reminiscent of Violet's, that from time to time he would find coiled upon his underwear when he was putting his laundry away, and how their presence posed a tender mystery he never attempted to solve or charge with meaning, wary of the trap of Keats's egotistical sublime. A narrow escape, since they could well have been hers.

"Now MORE are out," Albert tells Mills in the Eighth Street Marboro. Heads down, they had been slowly circling the long table of dollar remainders, Mills clock-wise, Albert counterclockwise, and gently collided. "Four in the chandelier, both coach lamps."

"Words, Albert, words," Mills says.

"Near darkness," Albert says.

Mills flips open a book. "I'm talking about *these*. All of them jammed in there. And there and there. We've been overrun with words, Albert. We're repeating ourselves."

"Dr. Johnson approved of the superfoetation of the press," Albert says.

"A man could still hope to read everything then. Now what do we have? Word pollution!" Mills slams the book shut, as though stemming the tide.

Albert says, "I once read about a prisoner who wanted to write a book but had nothing upon which to write it except the pages of a book, so he wrote in the spaces between the lines of print. This is interesting, but odd. On the face of it, one would more likely have paper than a pen or pencil. There are more sheets of paper in the world than writing instruments."

"Whether at a given time there are more blank sheets than ones densely covered with writing is problematical," Mills says.

"Besides," Albert says, "you would need an awful lot of pencils to write a book, and if you had access to a steady supply, it would seem that you could obtain writing paper, as well."

"To a lesser degree the same holds for ballpoints or ink for fountain or steel pens," Mills says.

"It could be, of course, that the prisoner wrote his book with, say, the bristles from his toothbrush dipped in his life's blood," Albert says.

"How much blood do you think it would take to write a decent-sized book?" Mills asks. "More than the five quarts in the human body?"

"Now, suppose the book he is so laboriously interlineating is one he himself wrote," Albert says. "Suppose further that it is autobiographical, as is the work in progress. In this case, he must resist the temptation to revise and amend his published volume, for if he does so at all extensively he will run out of room in which to write the new book. And being daily faced with the expression of old wastes, slack, and follies, his imperfect art like blighted acanthus leaves embellishing them, he must remember to turn aside when overcome, so that his tears don't dissolve what he has just written."

"We are in agreement then that his writing in pencil is farfetched," Mills says.

They decide to walk home together. It is evening, the air the blue of a black duck's speculum. On the way, Albert says, "To take it a step further, I have unresistingly become the prisoner of my own life. I have watched it close in, confine me, become as drab, uniform, and unyielding as the walls of a cell."

"Though conventionally narrow, the cell is immeasurably long," Mills says, "so from where you sit you cannot see either end."

"It is as though the book of my life were already written on an immense scroll in two crenellated lines of type, which immure me," Albert says.

"Prisoners traditionally write on the walls of their cells to those—or for those—who will come after them," Mills says. "If a prisoner were told that after he was executed his cell would be demolished, would he still write on the walls?"

"Yes, because he wouldn't believe them."

"That they were going to pull down his cell or that they were going to put him to death?"

Climbing the stoop, contemplating the lifeless coach lamps, Albert adds, "Insofar as I am imprisoned in the book of my life, which I am told will end (as I was told it began), I am, in effect, writing on the walls of my cell— merely, and compulsively, explicating my own text."

Mills opens the door. "Lenin exhorted, 'Ceaselessly explain,' " he says.

Flinging up an arm, like one of the beseeching figures in Titian's "Adoration," to draw Mills's attention to the chandelier, Albert cries out in the murky vestibule, "The public areas are your responsibility."

"And Ovid said," Mills goes on, " '*Scripta ferunt annos.*' "

ALBERT is awakened by the crash. At first, he imagines it is the shutter falling in the woods in Wellfleet; next, Mills slamming the book shut in Marboro.

"What happened?"

The question is as alarming as the crash. Once more Albert reaches out in the dark, reflecting that, having attained an age when his surroundings should be depressingly familiar, he seems increasingly to be feeling his way, whether toward momentous swimming pools or overmastering lilacs. And once again he encounters another man's wife.

He strives to look into the little bedroom, but he cannot see over the brow of the re-covered comforter, which, steadfast, folded in four, looms at the foot of the bed.

"Will you excuse me?" Albert says, getting up and heading into the little bedroom in his bare feet. He unexpectedly steps on earth. He crouches in the dark, fingering the damp soil, the cold fragments of the broken pot, the papery fronds. Extending a hand, he locates the pedestal table lying on its side, the place where one of the legs had snapped off. He must have set the pot down off center, and its unfailingly surprising weight, augmented by solicitous waterings, caused the leg to give way.

"What happened?" she says, crouching beside him, so that as he in turn picks up and lets drop the dirt, the shards, the fronds, he finds himself occasionally lifting her tumbling hair as though she, too, has come to grief.

"Shouldn't we stick it in something, or something?" she says.

A naked man and woman, Albert muses, huddled over a dying fern in the middle of the night as though re-enacting some ancestral sorrow—it's ten–twelve this affecting tableau has not been seen in New York since the turn of the century, when such affecting representations were more prevalent.

He dusts off his hands and rises. How quickly remorse is replaced by a sense of relief. Violet, his stepchildren, Josh, now the fern—one more thing he won't be encumbered by, have to take care of, be responsible for. Why is Violet weeping? When will Emily unlock her door? Is it true Barney put Josh in the refrigerator? Are the tips of the fronds dying in consequence of the great cycle of nature or because he is over-watering—or not watering enough? All that remains between him and seclusion, Albert realizes, are the philodendrons and the mushrooms.

"Oh, my God, what's that?" she says, having got up and bumped into what appears to be a severely stunted live oak festooned with Spanish moss. It is Albert's clothes dryer draped with socks. "Oh, it's a clothes dryer."

"Actually, it's a calendar," Albert says. "When I hang my socks up to dry, I count them and divide by two to discover how many days have gone by since I last washed them. Inevitably, more time has passed—or time has passed more quickly, I'm not sure it's the same thing—than I realized. A forcible reminder of the impermanence of our earthly mansions. By the same token, the Aztec Sun Stone, which archeologists believe to be a calendar, is in reality half of a giant waffle iron used on certain ceremonial occasions—the other half, which would make its purpose clear, being still unearthed."

So, too, Albert acknowledges, that while water, air, finally earth—or, everlastingly, fire—delineate us, we are molded and stamped by our responsibilities. The prospect of growing old among furled irises, raisinless bread, and slowly drying socks brings tears to Albert's eyes, which the other man's wife fails to detect, for Albert is now lying on the very edge of the bed—a habit he got into when he was married; that way, he could sleep with a hand on Josh's back to comfort him if he had bad dreams or awoke believing they had all gone away and left him.

After making sure she is asleep, Albert calls Violet.

"I just wanted to let you know that my life has become palindromic."

"Who am I speaking to?" Violet says.

"You are speaking to Albert, who is afraid his life makes as much sense backward as forward."

"Or as little," Violet says.

BECAUSE he has a lunch date, Albert goes to the Y before work instead of at noon and finds the pool full of old men and women—none, apparently, under seventy. They are swimming so slowly and in so many directions that he gets the impression they aren't making any progress, or, collaterally, that they have no destinations but are merely rocking back and forth like boats at their moorings. Like appalled Dante, Albert stares down at them from the deck. Except for the sound of an occasional wavelet breaking over the gutter, the pool is preternaturally silent; the swimmers' faces are composed, serene, their strokes and kicks so feeble or languorous they seem barely sufficient to keep them afloat.

"Do you get this bunch every morning?" Albert asks the lifeguard.

"From eight to twelve. Senior Citizens' A.M. Swim."

Taking note of the hours, Albert returns to the locker room; he will lower himself in at the shallow end twenty-five years hence.

ALBERT says, "Do gentile people always skip when they read?" He is unpacking, traipsing back and forth between the suitcase and the dresser, carrying a shirt or a little pile of underwear, as though putting away the costumes after another unsatisfactory performance of his life. The Human Dynamo is lying on her back on Albert's bed, holding an open book above her head, letting the pages slip one after another from under her right thumb, her arms uplifted, as were Michelangelo's on his scaffold and, as Walter Benjamin pointed out, Proust's upon his sickbed while holding his pages in the air. When Jews open a book, Albert reflects, they resolve—are condemned

—to read every word. But the mind strays, being suscep-
tible to such questions as why every now and again an
odd number of socks graces the clothes dryer and why it
is that no other creature except man can recall the past
at will.

EIGHT

~~~~~~~~~~~~~~~~~~~~~~~~~~~~

IN THE PREFACE TO *The Tragic Muse*, Henry James says that all we see of the artist in triumph "is the back he turns to us as he bends over his work." But what is our view of him in anything less than that state . . . ?

Albert lubricates the male ferrule with sebum from the side of his nose, and puts his spinning rod together. He fits the reel foot into the rod seat, twists the retainer rings and screws them down tight. Then he strips out the seventeen-pound test mono, gently threads it through the guides, and checks the line for frays and nicks. He slips the line through a one-ounce egg sinker and the eye of a snap swivel, twists it five times, passes it through the loop formed by the first twist, and draws it tight. Next he opens the swivel and slips the snell loop of a wire-snelled 7/o long-shank bluefish hook into the swivel and snaps it shut. He fixes the hook in an envelope upon which "Compliments of Mr. Al E. Mohny" is written and goes to his bedroom window. Opening the bail, he lowers the rig into the garden three stories below, where Violet is sitting with Skippy Mountjoy.

Paying out the line, Albert reflects on the contingencies awaiting all of us. For example, having recently purchased his first pair of reading glasses, he discovered the other night that he had inadvertently worn them while masturbating.

WHEN she has calmed down, the Human Dynamo declares that the only conceivable reason Albert told Violet the garden apartment was available was that he had run out of material. She tells this to him on the telephone toward the end of a long, heroic, even Wagnerian conversation. Because the Human Dynamo lives in New Canaan and Albert in New York, they talk on the phone nearly every night, largely about what she had for dinner and whether he needs to bring bread.

In the winter, Albert visits the Human Dynamo Wednesdays, because she skis weekends; in the summer, he visits her Saturdays, because on weekdays she plays tennis after work until it is too dark to see the ball. When he tells her their relationship is absurd, she says, "Why don't you take up tennis [or skiing], so we could have fun together?" Do you know Donatello's "Dead Christ with Angels"? One of the piteous, attending cherubs has clapped a chubby hand to its cheek—nowadays, curiously, a gesture associated with Jewish people, as the Human Dynamo calls us. This is Albert's attitude when he is told he should take up tennis (or skiing) at forty-six.

Because the Human Dynamo doesn't eat bread, she considers it extravagant to buy a whole loaf so Albert can have toast for breakfast on Thursday (winter) or Sunday (summer). If she goes to her parents for dinner, she filches a slice for him; otherwise, he has to bring one with him on the train, wrapping it in foil and slipping it into his jacket pocket.

Like other clandestine acts, carrying a concealed slice of bread is to a degree thrilling, and invests the bearer with a sense of mission, self-importance, and romance. Returning to his office from the Y one Wednesday afternoon, Albert reckons he may be the only person walking the streets of New York with a slice of Sprouted Wheat in his pocket. Chances are that at that very moment more bombs are being conveyed in this fashion, and with the terrorist, Albert shares the unendurable need to let someone in on the secret.

"Excuse me, sir. Perhaps you've noticed this slight bulge in my pocket. Pat it for a moment and see if you can guess what I have in here?"

"A paperback?"

"No."

"An eight-track of The Grateful Dead?"

"Uh-uh."

"A very small ant farm?"

When Albert informs the Human Dynamo that as a consequence of reminding him to bring bread or, for example, asking him to solve such moral dilemmas as whether she has the right to insist that Kurt, a BMW dealer and former beau with whom she is dickering for a new car, throw in cocoa mats, his phone bills are averaging more than a hundred dollars a month, she says, "I'm worth it. You give *her* five hundred dollars a month."

ALBERT also gives Violet his dying quince. Unlike the alimony checks, he doesn't lower the branches from his window on fishing line, but carefully carries them downstairs, avoiding the sprinkler system, as though he were participating in a multilevel production of *Macbeth*, so they won't shed petals all over the runners. Violet has told him she can't afford fresh flowers because her lawyer let Albert's lawyer—his father, *her* ex-father-in-law—put one over by not taking into account the fact that she has to pay taxes on her alimony, so that instead of getting five hundred a month, she only gets two hundred and eighty-three dollars and thirty-three cents. Whatever, Albert recalls that when he was married to her, the apartment was full of moribund chrysanthemums and asters standing in dark, faintly fetid water. Albert often wondered why she didn't get rid of them. Was it because of neglect or because of a yearning for the wild, rank, and tangled associated with her rural upbringing? "Willows, old rotten planks, slimy posts and brickwork, I love such things." Constable was another such fancier.

Once Albert threw out several boughs that were so ancient they had come to resemble antlers, being covered with a velvetlike growth. When Violet learned what he had done, she burst into tears; the branches were from the magnolia that grew beside the house in which she had been born, and she had broken them off for a memento when it was put up for sale. Their marriage had been characterized by such sensational episodes, as had that of her parents. Following Violet's appearance on the kitchen table, upon which stage her nine older brothers and sisters had previously made their entrances, the midwife, piqued that Violet's father had been so heedless as to make his wife suffer through ten pregnancies one after the other, thrust the afterbirth at him, which he flung in the fireplace. Albert has tried to imagine what *his* dad's reaction would have been if he had been handed his, Albert's, afterbirth.

To make up for putting the magnolia down the incinerator, Albert bought Violet a print of a sprig of small magnolia, or white bay. This now hangs with other floral prints above her bed. Whenever Albert comes bearing his old quince—or, at other seasons, forsythia, dogwood, pendulous, ashen lilacs—and puts the branches in a vase by her fireplace, Scotch-taping them to the mantelpiece so they won't tip the vase over, he notices anew that the prints are hanging crooked. This disarray is especially poignant. When he and Violet were married, he kept the pictures straight; now their obliquity seems to him symbolic of her inability to cope without him and gives rise to tender sentiments, though she might very well be unaware that the prints are dazzlingly crooked, considering rectitude unimportant.

This last reflection gives Albert pause. He visualizes himself going critically about his apartment, nudging prints of walruses, flounders, and orioles into line; making sure the telephone sits squarely on the telephone table, but a little off center to improve the composition; and arranging the overlapping magazines on the coffee table so that they describe a gentle, jagged arc. In the right angles he recognizes his dad's influence, in the curves his mom's.

During the eleven years of his marriage, Albert tried to instill in his stepchildren this sense of order and fitness, this artistic vision, if you will. He believes he had failed, as he had in inculcating his store of practical and moral precepts, until the other evening when Emily, who is now twenty-three, came to dinner. While waiting for her ice cream "to turn to mush," she wandered about the living room. "Your dictionary is open to 'p,' " she suddenly announced. Although her tone was gloating, Albert had the impulse to take her in his arms. How many times had he told her and Barney to leave the dictionary open to "m" after looking something up? *It had sunk in!* Solicitously kneading her ice cream with a tablespoon, which keeps getting bent out of shape, so that he has to keep straightening it (surely a parallel can be drawn with the examined life), Albert recalls his dad's explanation, which he had automatically passed on—what did he know of physics?—that the spine would be ruined if the dictionary was left open to any letter other than "m," especially those at the beginning or end of the alphabet. *Ruined!* How often his dad had invoked that fate, whether in respect to Albert's posture as a result of slouching about all over the place, or to the chairs he insisted on tipping back at the dinner table.

Albert goes over to the dictionary and clutches it with both hands, his left thumb on the page headed "Mainstay," his right on the one headed "Make," the fingers of his left hand on "Collegium," those of his right on "Tortive," as though passionately grasping two hanks of hair to force a lover's head closer or, as he had done years ago, to fling his disobedient stepdaughter from him.

Albert stands before the dictionary, shaking it, as if once and for all to put his dad's theory to the test or to punish the words, to scatter them into unintelligibility for failing to serve him, for not bending to his will— or to express his ardor for them.

It has been said that words are stones, compact and uncompromising, picked up from civilization's communal rubble, hacked out of its great, repetitive designs; it has been said that words are bright, lightly tossing buoys, marking definitions lying far below. In the first case, writing is like building a wall; in the second, it is a series of deep, baffling dives. And it has been said (by Jung) that words butter no parsnips.

"What are you doing?" Emily says apprehensively.

What *is* he doing? Albert releases his hold and smooths out the pages, as though the dictionary were a pillow upon which he would later gratefully lay his head.

But I left Albert fishing from the window. Surely, no angler will have better luck. It is gusty, darkening, early spring. The air through which the white envelope —addressor Mr. Al E. Mohny—flutters down is palest lavender, the color, Albert recalls from his life with Violet, that cornflowers turn if they're not thrown out. She and Skippy are seated at a glass-topped table, in which overarching California privet is reflected, the images of the tossing branches more tempestuous than their actual counterparts, either because they are concentrated, like a stormy sea funnelled against rocks, or because an image is in a sense art, which heightens. Drinking iced tea, Violet and Skippy are unaware of the descending envelope, now hovering ominously a few feet above their heads.

As Skippy begins laughing—immoderate laughter that from time to time awakens Albert in the middle of the night—the telephone rings. Albert turns the reel handle to snap the bail shut, lays the rod on the floor, and answers the phone. It's the Human Dynamo, who left the courts early on account of the wind. "Should I name my car 'Yogurt'?" she says.

She explains that she is going to register her new BMW in Vermont so she won't have to pay the local property tax, and is thinking of getting vanity plates.

"It can't be more than six characters."

"Have you considered anything else?"

" 'Sundae,' 'Banana,' 'Raisin,' 'Gopher,' 'Muffin.' "

"Does it have to be comestible or small and furry?"

" 'Squeak,' 'Oh Wow,' 'Breezy.' What do you think, Albie?"

"I think we ought to get a WATS line."

"No, *really*."

"I *really* think you should call it 'Virtue,' after your age."

"Huh?"

"The ancients regarded twenty-eight as the perfect number because it equals the sum of all its divisors and therefore signifies virtue. I think a good many motorists would find it uplifting."

"Do you think you're too old for me?"

"I think I'm too old for myself," Albert says, imagining

driving along the South Dixie Highway in the prolonged summer twilight, his plates emblazoned MISERY or CRISIS or SORROW.

After he's hung up, Albert returns to the window and begins reeling in. By then it is dark, the wind has died; Violet and Skippy are either sitting quietly under the privet or have gone inside. Albert has the impression that while he was on the phone, line had been taken out and that he is fishing in an abyss. What had he expected to catch? To what use could he put a fragment of the past? Aubrey wrote of seeing a mower using an arm off the monument of a lord in a ruined abbey nearby to whet his scythe.

"WHILE preparing my income tax," Albert's dad, who is now eighty, says, "I was made aware of a haunting fragrance."

"I think 'haunting' is too theatrical for daisies," Albert's mom says, biting into a brownie. "Jasmine. Frangipani—"

"I think 'was made' is too literary, particularly for the Upper West Side," Albert says. "What's wrong with 'became'? I became aware—"

"I have become aware that I am surrounded by *petit stinquers*," his dad says, frenchifying, his habit in a tight spot.

Albert is having dinner at his parents', which he does every Friday.

"At any rate," his dad goes on, "the fragrance unexpectedly wafted across my calculations. I looked up, puzzled. It was—" He indicates the daisies, which, with an arrangement of gourds, make up the centerpiece. "It was evocative."

Albert waits for him to say of what, but his dad's lips are compressed. He turns to his mom to see if there is a secret and she shares it. She, too, is looking at him expectantly. Albert detects that she is on the verge of smiling, but is unsure whether it would be appropriate. In the moments in which his dad is apparently dwelling on the evocation the scent of daisies gave rise to and his mom is evidently trying to again come to terms with the fact that the man to whom she has been married for more than fifty years has memories of idyllic interludes from which she is forever excluded, Albert recalls reeling in his line until the bare hook appeared above the sill.

"Jake's coming back," he announces to change the subject.

"Jake?" his mom says.

"Josh's litter brother," Albert says.

"They're those dogs," his dad says to his mother.

Shortly after they were married, Albert and Violet had bought two dachshund puppies, Josh and Jake. When they were four, Jake inexplicably began attacking Josh. Albert and Violet decided they would have to separate them, and advertised to find a new home for Jake. The ad was answered by a childless couple named White. Albert took Jake in a taxi to their apartment in the West Eighties, in which rows of nearly identical cacti were set out beneath indistinct landscapes featuring morose cows. Albert showed Mr. White, a short man with a frequent, perhaps facetious laugh, how to clean Jake's ears; he hadn't seen him since. Josh now lived with Violet, as I've mentioned. In the morning, when Albert went for the *Times*, he took Josh along, forgotten down by his ankles; when he delivered his withering bouquets, he would dandle him on his knees, like the infant he never had, contemplating the greying muzzle, preposterous in this context, scarred by Jake's teeth: part dog, part child, part god.

"I began to have pangs," Albert tells his parents. "I felt I had cast Jake out of my life, disposed of him. I wanted to see him again before he died. I called the Whites up. Dialling, I had a premonition I would be too late. Mrs. White answered. 'How's that 'ittle doggie doin' after all these years?' I said. 'He's fine,' she said. 'He was a great comfort to Mr. White at the end.' It turned out the 'ittle hubbie had died three years ago. I didn't know what to say. I was entranced by the irony. The upshot is she's going to Corfu for ten days and would be delighted to have Jake visit me while she's away."

"For the life of me, I don't know why you go out of your way to encumber yourself," his mom says.

"You persist in dwelling in the past," his dad says.

"Installing Violet right under your feet," his mom says. "How are you ever to go forward?"

"I seem to be swept along," Albert says. "I'm going to be in *Who's Who*."

"In the Northeast?" his dad says. "I'm in the Northeast. *Who's Who in the Northeast*. I've been in there for ages."

"*In America*," Albert says, feeling that it may be an uncharitable remark.

"I'm in the morgue," his dad says.

"I'm in the morgue, too," his mom says.

Albert envisages the two slim manila envelopes of brittle, yellowing clippings nestled side by side in a filing cabinet, closer than their subjects are in life.

"I'm clearing the decks," Albert's dad says abruptly,

rising, as though realizing that in weighing his accomplishments he had kept his thumb on the scale and that there is no time to lose if he wants to swell his envelope. He begins scooping up plates.

"I'll do it," Albert's mom says, also rising.

They face each other warily across the littered table like wrestlers before a match.

"I'm restoring some order," his dad says.

"You're terrible," his mom says.

"You're the second person who's called me that today."

"Who was the first?" she says.

"Albert's Violet."

"I never—"

"I was riding the down escalator at the bank, when I noticed her rising toward me on the up escalator. I greeted her. 'You're a terrible man,' she said."

"I never—"

"I wanted to ask her what she meant, but we were rapidly drawing apart. When I reached the bottom I got on the up escalator. When I reached the top she had vanished. Albert, do you have any idea what she meant?"

"The tax on the alimony, probably."

"But she was represented."

"I never—"

"Please sit down," Albert says. "*I'm* going to clear the table."

"Do you think I'm terrible?" his dad asks, slowly lowering himself, reaching behind with one hand, as though uncertain whether his chair might have been whisked away, that his life might have turned out to be some sort of practical joke.

"Violet tends to divide people into friendlies and hostiles," Albert says. "I believe it has to do with coming from a large family where you had to fight for hind teat." Once again he imagines his dad, a young man not unlike himself at thirty-three, but appalled, not knowing what to do with his, Albert's, afterbirth.

"It's not your dad's fault that she didn't have better representation," Albert's mom says.

Albert collects the teacups and heads for the kitchen.

"Don't dispose of the lemon," his dad sings out. "There are one or two squeezes left."

"Why don't you take more dishes with you?" his mom calls after him. "Then you won't have to make so many trips."

Pushing open the swinging door, Albert thinks: But I want to keep going back and forth; that way I can postpone whatever is going to happen next: e.g., that the last of the argyle socks Violet bought him during the course of their marriage and sedulously darned would get a hole in it and he would have to throw it out. Albert thinks of himself as a balloon, whose mooring lines are being cast off one by one, so that one day he will unexpectedly, fearfully, stately rise.

RETURNING from his parents, Albert runs into Skippy Mountjoy walking Josh.

"What was the blue-plate special tonight?" Skippy asks, falling in alongside him. "Roast capon or brisket?"

"Know my every move, don't you, Skippy?"

"Josh clues me. Dog's very deep. Ver-ry deep. Ver-ry 'ittle gets by 'ittle Josh. Fridays Mom and Dad, Saturdays Human Dynamo, except in the winter when it's Wednesdays and the Knicks are Saturdays, as well as Tuesdays, when they're at home. Josh tells me Jake's coming for a visit. Think they'll mix it up?"

"No. Jake was always the aggressor. I'm convinced it had to do with territory. Josh never had a sense of territory. Besides, the territory no longer exists."

"Care to draw any parallels vis-à-vis you, me, and Violet?"

"Only if you do, Skippy."

"Oh, no, I pass. Never touch the stuff. More in your line—analogizing, metaphorizing. No izing on my cake. Right, Josh? Dog's got unimagined depths. You, you've got imagined depths. Right, Albie? Surface another story."

They pass beneath the sycamores that border the sidewalk at intervals, treading on the fretted shadows of their foliage. Albert has the impression the shadows are duckweed and that they are walking on water.

"What do you mean?"

"You're in a rut."

"I'm not in a rut, Skippy. I lead a contrived life."

"V-8, schav, three-quarters of a pound of ground round, Sprouted Wheat and applesauce every night is a poor contrivance, then. Allow me to give you my recipe for red-wine court bouillon."

They have reached the gate to the three steps leading to Violet's apartment. Skippy unlatches it and Josh bounds down. Albert turns to climb the stoop. Taking out his keys, he tells Skippy, "Send it up on the line sometime."

As he approaches his landing, Albert hears his telephone ringing. He pounds up the remaining stairs, unlocks the door, and runs for the phone.

"It's me." It's the Human Dynamo.

"Yes, what is it?" Albert says, out of breath.

"Oh, Albert, a bird pooped on my new car."

WHEN Albert gets into bed, he puts on his glasses, but doesn't read. Instead, he wonders whether by nature the contrived life precludes what were once called "the good parts"; e.g., "This book has a lot of good parts" or "Did you get to the good parts yet?" If he puts a quarter in a Times Square peep show, invariably an innocuous segment of the loop appears; a blonde and a brunette in a convertible driving along a palm-lined street, making little *moues* as they try to find the house where the mixed foursome will take place. Albert is almost convinced that no matter how many quarters he spends, he will never get to see the good parts, that in episode after episode the girls will continue to circle through the streets, becoming more and more fretful —the acting here godawful—at their inability to find the right address, that it will gradually become dark, the lights come on, the girls' eyes, the convertible gleaming lustrously beneath the palms. . . .

Albert takes off his glasses and folds the earpieces. They make two little clicks when they strike the frames. He is charmed by the sound. What a satisfactory way to denote the conclusion of yet another day, like the detonation of a remote sunset gun. To think that until recently his days ended unceremoniously. In a sense, these minute, faintly melancholy salutes constitute good parts, too, he supposes.

Several hours later, Albert's bedroom door opens. The light from the landing discloses a little boy of two or so. He is wearing a brown velveteen suit. A spray of quince and leather-leaf fern is pinned to his lapel. He makes a hieratic sign. "Behold," he says, "I show you a mystery."

As he totters toward the bed, Albert sees that his eyes are red, glowing, like a dog's in a flash photograph.

"Jakie!"

Extending his arms, Albert recalls walking him and Josh, how they vibrantly anchored him to the ground, gave him a sense of place and intention.

The next morning, Albert is awakened by the phone.

"It's me." It's Violet.

"Yes, what is it?"

"Oh, Albert, a squirrel's eating my babies'-breath."

"It has been said that the greatest single discovery in the history of thought is the invention of a symbol for nought," Albert says. He is sitting at Violet's desk, writing out her alimony check. "It would make a nice couplet, if I worked at it."

"We would've made a nice couple if you had worked at it," Violet says, Scotch-taping to her mantlepiece the quince he brought downstairs. She steps back to examine her handiwork. As if on cue, a few pink petals flutter pathetically to the hearth. "And if it's such a great invention, why don't you add another to the check?"

"I hear you passed my dad on an escalator and called him a terrible man," Albert says, taking off his shoes and climbing up on Violet's bed.

"Because he is."

Albert straightens the floral prints above her pillows, then begins jumping up and down on the bed.

"Violet, do I look like a high-bouncing ex-lover?"

"You look like someone who has shafted me."

"I'll set up an appointment for you with my accountant. Maybe he can scheme up some deductions."

"Timmmberrrr!" Violet cries.

On the way up, Albert sees the Scotch tape ripping loose, the quince going over. He springs off the bed, catching the branches before they bring the vase down. The last of the blossoms litter the hearth.

" 'In a drear-nighted December,' " Albert quotes, picking them up, "Too happy, happy tree/Thy branches ne'er remember/Their green felicity.' I have to go."

"It's Saturday, isn't it?"

"I'm catching the five-oh-five."

"Don't go. When you're here, I think of you up there. It's like you're sitting on my head. When you're away, I have no top."

"But it's Saturday."

He backs toward the door, the blossoms filling his cupped palms, not knowing where to put them.

"Albert," Violet says, holding out her hands, "why don't you take up bowling so we can have fun together?"

He gently tips the petals into her hands.

Albert hears the telephone ringing as he climbs the stairs.

"It's me." It's the Human Dynamo. She's sobbing.

"What's wrong?"

"The form came from the Vermont Motor Vehicle Bureau."

"And—"

"And Albie, it says you're only allowed to have *five* characters."

"And—"

"And all I can think of is 'Peach.' I had such good names for my car."

"We'll discuss it at dinner."

"Don't forget to bring bread."

ON THE five-oh-five he reinvisages the South Dixie Highway at twilight. This time his plates bear ENNUI, GUILT. A few miles beyond Port Chester, the train comes to a halt. Five or ten minutes pass and there is still no announcement about pantographs or stalled trains ahead. Then the doors slide open. Several passengers, Albert among them, jump to the ground and walk forward along the roadbed. It is a mild, clear evening. The engineer and the conductors are standing in front of the head car, gazing down. Joining them, Albert sees that they are at the rim of a vast abyss. Its interior is largely in shadow, the very depths filled with a bluish haze out of which protrude vividly colored eminences of sandstone and shale, suggesting minarets, turrets, steeples, spires. Albert pictures the Human Dynamo waiting forlornly at the station in her new BMW. If he can descend into the abyss and then scale the other side, he can get a cab at Greenwich.

He lowers himself over the edge and plunges down a rocky slope. After he has gone a way, he looks back. He can no longer see the rim. Raising his eyes higher, as though contemplating a Tiepolo ceiling, he descries not whirling, apotheosizing figures but a cloudless sky being drained of light. He continues picking his way down; on the more level stretches the little evening primrose *Oenothera pterosperma* displays its pink blossoms. My life has been one long interruption, he muses, between what I intended to do and what I never got around to doing. While composing "Intimations," Wordsworth was interrupted by the arrival of Mr. Olliff's load of dung, and went to work in the garden. But he finished it.

Slipping and sliding on the scree in his suède loafers, Albert loses his footing and fetches up against a hoodoo. Brushing himself off, he discovers he is carrying something in his jacket pocket. What does he have in there? A pack of cigars? A bundle of love letters? A well-folded Speedo swimsuit? He fishes out the object and unwraps it. For some unfathomable reason, a slice of bread.

NINE

~~~~~~~~~~~~~~~~~~

ALBERT ONCE KNEW a woman who designed women's gloves. Paper cutouts of hands—left or right, he couldn't tell which; either sufficed—were strewn throughout her apartment. At another time, he went with a woman who did illustrations for advertisements of women's shoes. Her apartment was littered with shoes—one of a kind, left or right; she had no need for pairs. While Albert was married, the apartment in which he and Violet lived was awash with tears. Like subatomic particles whose existence is confirmed by photographs of their tracks, the fugitive existence of these tears was often made evident to Albert only by the rapidly drying streaks on his wife's cheeks. The tears, he noted, had trickled from her left eye as well as her right. "Being married to you," she once told him, "you need both barrels."

Albert and Violet have been separated for three years. During the first two, her tears had dried up, the transeunt cause, himself, having been removed, although not very far. Indeed, separation is a particularly apt word to describe their situation, Albert living, as I have previously noted, on the third, and top, floor, Violet in the garden apartment.

From his bedroom window Albert can look down into the garden, which he has paid a young man who hoped to serve mankind by combining ecology with the law to do over, as Violet's forty-eighth-birthday present. This humanitarian cut back the privet and planted Hosta beneath it, uprooted a large ailanthus in favor of a crab apple, and put in a bed of annuals, a border of day lilies, a rosebush that never leafed, much less budded, and, at Violet's insistence, several tomato plants. He told her these were going to be very iffy, because the garden got so little sun, but Violet was adamant. The great contending themes of her life were a yearning for her rustic upbringing and *nostalgie de la boue*; in this case the former held sway.

As predicted, the tomato plants fared poorly; further, they were ravaged by squirrels. Skippy Mountjoy, who came by to work on his sonnet sequence under the privet, enclosed the plants with chicken wire, but the squirrels swarmed up and over the netting. He then laid a heavy cardboard poster of Dürer's "Feast of the Rose Garlands" on top of the wire enclosure. This kept the squirrels out but plunged the plants into near-total darkness.

As far as Albert can tell, the poster has never served a decorative purpose. Violet told him that when Barney was an infant it had been used as a gate to keep him from tumbling downstairs. While Albert was married to Violet, they had penned in Josh and Jake with it. Now, when Albert gazes out his bedroom window, what catches his eye is this weather-beaten *Rosenkranzbild*, resplendent with the roses the nearby bush never produced. The poster is askew, Skippy not having aligned it to be viewed from Albert's vantage.

Albert tells Violet on the phone one day, "If that thing's going to hit me in the eye every morning when I open the curtains, the least you can do is straighten it out."

"That's just like you," she says. "You're not satisfied having the world spread out at your feet, it has to be at right angles."

Notwithstanding, Albert shortly sees Violet go into the garden. "To the left!" he shouts out the window. "A little more. More. Too much. Back to the right. Hold it!"

Albert reflects that he and Violet are communicating at longer and longer range. While a few years ago they were murmuring in one another's ears, now they speak on the phone, shout out windows, leave notes for each other under the carpet in Unit 40 of the Sun 'n Sea Motel on Key Biscayne. Albert and Violet had honeymooned there fifteen years before and have often gone back since; now, of course, they go to Florida separately, but they cling to their old unit. When neither of them is there, Albert envisions solitary middle-aged men like himself doing push-ups on the carpet, spent lovers out-flung upon it as though they have fallen from great heights, the maids raking it to make the nap stand up, all unaware of the tender messages beneath them, and he is put in mind of the numberless generations of Anatolian herdsmen and charcoal burners who have gone about their business ignorant of the poems, correspondence, and bills of lading impressed into clay tablets that have lain buried for millennia under their feet.

At times, Albert stands by his open window at night, singing "Da-da-da." (According to the Human Dynamo, when Jewish people don't know the words to songs they go "da-da," while gentiles go "la-la." She is given to this kind of generalization. Violet is a generalizer, too, although of a different sort; e.g., "The reason you don't have any friends is that you don't really like people. You just like those parts of them that suit your purposes. Which is why all of us who became involved with you are maimed." Why is it, Albert thinks, that I, who never draw inferences, invariably wind up in the dark with my arms around women who make generalizations?)

Sometimes, as Albert stands and sings, the dark garden seems to him to be flooded, with just the topmost branches of the privet projecting from the water, and the blistered poster a raft upon which a desperate swimmer might try to haul himself, only to find it wouldn't support the weight of a child. A notion comes to him: except for those Bibles in which bullets become embedded, works of art don't save lives.

In the morning, as Albert looks down into the garden while waiting for Violet to answer the phone, it seems to have dwindled overnight, withered, as though time has suddenly tightened its grip, or that he is viewing it from higher up than the third story, from that fancied height which the imagined lovers he has envisioned on the motel carpet have cast themselves.

"Elite," Albert says when Violet picks up the receiver. This is short for Elite Dog-Walking Service and means that he is coming downstairs to walk Josh. Similarly, Skippy Mountjoy is the Acme Dog-Walking Service, or Acme, it being his pleasure to take Josh out between *abab* and *cdcd*.

One autumn morning, when Albert arrives to walk Josh, he becomes aware of a pungent, almost acrid odor he can't identify. Although not that of burning leaves, it correspondingly stirs the emotions, evoking pathetic feelings and a sense of impermanence—*lacrimae rerum*.

"What's cooking?" Albert asks Violet.

"Credit cards," she says from the bathroom.

Albert enters. She is sitting in the tub, in several inches of soapy water, dreamily shaving her legs; Josh is curled on the bathmat. She is rosy, and the water has a bluish tinge, the blue of infants' veins, and gently heaves with her motions. Vapor has condensed on the medicine-cabinet mirror, so that Albert can't find his reflection. The airport is closed in, the plane is in a holding pattern, and he is unable to see out the bleary window. During the last years of their marriage, this had seemed an appropriate metaphor, and, in a sense, he is still waiting for permission to land. Now the amplitude of gentle curves —Violet bending to her shins, Josh on the bathmat, the bell graph of his life—nearly brings him to tears.

"They're ashes," Violet says.

Ah! He recalls the four of them crowded about the stove, Barney and Emily taking turns holding an expired Master Charge in the flame, raptly watching it blacken, melt, blister, vanish. Families have these rites or ceremonies. Another of theirs had been the watering of the fern: the procession to the bathroom to "The Washington Post" march ("la-la"s from Violet, Emily, and Barney;

"da-da"s from Albert); the lowering of the fern into the tub (all hum "Taps"); and the spraying. This last had been enhanced by manipulating the plastic sprayer so that it emitted an uncannily human moan, which sent the children into peals of laughter.

"I'm consolidating my position," Violet says.

"What?" He isn't paying attention. Despite their ministrations, the fern hadn't flourished. Like tea leaves in the bottom of a cup, adumbrating pinnules littered the tub. Kneeling before it after the others had borne the fern away, Albert devotedly gathered them up and, as his dad would say, disposed of them.

"They were too much of a temptation," Violet is saying. "I can't afford them anymore. American Express, Visa, Master Charge—I consigned them to the flames, as your father would say. How is your father, by the way? Is he still being oracular?"

"Yesterday he told me there were seventeen chairs in his proctologist's waiting room. I said, 'You counted them?' He said, 'I did.' 'But why?' 'It helped pass the time. Didn't I ever tell you about my propensity for enumerating?' I said he hadn't, and what else did he count? 'Members of orchestras,' he told me. I expressed my amazement, and was forced to reconsider all the time I had spent in his company. Untold occasions when he must have been secretly totting things up swam into view. 'There's a lot about me you don't know,' he said."

"But you," Violet says, "you're an open book, aren't you?"

Tugging Josh along Sixth Avenue, Albert tries to recall if he has ever represented himself that way. An open book is not like an open door or a disrobed woman; for all practical purposes, it discloses only two pages, a fraction of its contents, and the odds are against these being in themselves particularly revelatory—"the axe," as Kafka said, describing the proper function of books, "for the frozen sea inside us." Masturbatory practices aside, Albert wonders whether he leads a secret life. (The Human Dynamo once inquired of him whether, in fact, he even led what is commonly construed as a *life*. It was late at night and they were in Forest Hills, walking along a leafy, deserted street to her BMW, he having prevailed upon her to leave the stadium in the middle of the fourth set of an interminable baseline match between Vilas and Orantes which threatened to end at daybreak. It proved to be an unpopular move. "When was the last time you examined your motives?" she shrieked. "Have you ever considered the consequences of your acts? What is your guiding principle? Never to venture more than a hundred yards from a bathroom?" Albert didn't reply. He was concentrating on avoiding her handbag, which she was swinging at his head. He was a practiced hand, in his marriage to Violet having dodged hard rolls, tangerine sections, and a platter of linguine with white clam sauce.)

Shortly after Albert leaves Josh off and returns to his apartment, he notices that Skippy is in the garden. The perspective is unsettling, like that of Raphael's "The Glorification of the Sacrament" or Mantegna's "The Dead Christ," and brings to mind the view from the roof of the dome of St. Peter's, to which he climbed years ago. From there, the great statues of the saints—which, when looking up at them from below, he assumed to be erect—appeared, like swimmers on the mark, to be on the verge of launching themselves into the square. So much depends on one's vantage point, Albert reflects—where you are standing. We rely on conventions, the way things are supposed to be, for most of our understanding, and thus tend to skip the hard parts—endeavoring to find hidden truths, to elucidate mysteries, to recognize a cry for help; even the road to self-knowledge becomes paved. In this respect, poets are no more often seen from above than whales from below, until someone wields Kafka's splintering axe.

Albert takes up the binoculars with which he watches birds, and trains them on Skippy's notebook to see if he can make out what he is writing. Albert reads: "The perusal of literary compositions across a state line, with intent to appropriate them for one's own use, is a Federal offense, punishable by no less than . . ."

Withdrawing from the window, Albert goes to the bathroom. Above the tub is a skylight. As though he is in the Pantheon or Texas Stadium, a shaft of sunlight some-times unexpectedly illuminates him while he is taking a shower, and he feels as if he is being singled out . . . but for what? Lately, Albert has come to the conclusion that if it it possible to absorb the unhappiness of others, that will be the mission he will undertake. Like the old-clothes man who in his youth trudged the streets, head expectantly up-lifted, crying "Old clothes! Old clothes!" and retrieved the bundles that housewives flung from the windows, he will cry out "Sorrows! Sorrows!" and wait below with open arms.

"Fire!" a voice cries, awakening Albert and the Human Dynamo, who is sleeping over. He gets out of bed and rushes downstairs. The vestibule seems to be ablaze, and a black youth of sixteen or so is dancing wildly about the flames. When Albert gets closer, he sees that what is burning is a stack of firewood that Mills keeps behind the front door, and what the boy is doing is trying to grab some of the fiery logs so he can throw them onto the sidewalk. Albert joins in, but the flames are too intense; in addition, the wall against which the wood is stacked has caught fire. Recalling that the hose used to flush the sidewalk is hooked on the top rung of the ladder leading to the basement, Albert runs down the stoop, heaves open the basement doors, and passes the hose up to the boy. When the fire is out and the boy (was he a firebug?) gone, Albert turns to put the hose away and notices for the first time that the Human Dynamo is standing on the sidewalk. Alongside her, but somewhat apart, is Violet, wearing a robe that his mother had insisted on giving him but that he had had no use for; Skippy Mountjoy, dressed in an old raincoat of Albert's that Violet had altered and given to Skippy; and Josh, whose leash Skippy is holding. Looking down at them from the top of the stoop, Albert is struck by how short, even stumpy, Violet and Skippy are compared to the Human Dynamo and himself. It is almost as if they are members of a different race—one among which, like an anthropologist or missionary, he has dwelt but whose mysteries he hasn't penetrated; they are sharers in a tribal history from which he is excluded. His hand-me-downs seem to point up his own inadequacies; they wear them the way savages wear top hats—not for their civilizing effects but for panache.

They stand motionless, expressionless, staring at him, as though about to be photographed on the banks of a tributary of the Orinoco. Towering above them, Albert feels that something is expected of him. Again, what? To take notes? To forgive them? To allow *them* to forgive *him*? The Human Dynamo, for her part, is looking at him as if to say, After tagging along all these years, is this my reward—an obscure confrontation in the smoky, reeking dark? Have you dragged me here to be a witness to your failure to involve yourself with people?

Albert's eyes are tearing—not, he feels, from emotion this time, but from the smoke, whose volumes rise all about him. He is on the verge of disappearing, he thinks, or rather they are. Although he can now begin all over again, a long, dark line, like that scorched in the grass by a powder train, will inescapably connect him with the past.

There is a momentary rent in the smoke, revealing Josh. How old and scuffy he is, like Barney's football, which had been kicked around the P. S. 41 schoolyard for years. Albert realizes he has not paid Josh much attention since becoming separated from Violet; the dog is merely a vague presence down there at the end of the leash, a warm, trusting neck about which Albert fastens and unfastens a collar. Had he neglected Barney in the same way?

"Josh is losing his fuzz," Albert says to Violet.

"Acme had nowhere to stay, Elite," he hears Violet say.

This time, the stench of ashes reminds Albert of dead campfires, and thus of summer camp and his youth—the woods sloping down to the lake, the blue foothills on the far shore, which he never reached, the bluer mountains beyond. These unattained peaks at times come to mind when he goes downstairs in the morning to take Josh for a walk. Albert invariably finds him asleep in the chair by Violet's bed, and he gropes for him in the dark among the folds of his blanket, trying to determine which is Josh's front end, which his rear. While doing so, he glances at the bed, and is reassured by the gentle swell of the covers that indicate Violet's sleeping form; it is a landmark that enables him to maintain his bearings, to complete the familiar circle of his horizon. But some mornings another range—steeper, more massive, jagged—looms behind her, as though the earth has shifted overnight and new features have been upthrust.

In these instances, when Josh is following him to the kitchen for his biscuit, Albert often comes upon the visitor's shoes. They are slip-ons—large, black, scuffed. Usually, one will be upright, one on its side, and they are never together; Albert has the impression that they have been kicked off in an access of passion or that their wearer has met a violent end—an explosion, a hit-and-run.

It is Albert's practice on weekends to buy the *Times*, a brioche, and a bunch of flowers while walking Josh, and to leave them, agreeably arranged, on Violet's dining-room table. Whenever he sees in her bed what looms like a toppling wave or the greater half of a dictionary unequally open, he buys an extra brioche. For some reason, the addition of a second roll poses an almost insuperable obstacle to putting together a satisfactory still life, and he will stand in the dining room for long minutes, fussing with its components. Once he recalled his mom's dismay upon glancing at his and his dad's dinner plates. "I've turned the asparagus the wrong way!" she had cried. Holding the extra brioche aloft, as though it is a chess piece he isn't sure where to set down—or, indeed, if it is the right piece to move—Albert thinks, Perhaps I am better suited to be a mother. Indeed, toward the end of the marriage the roles were ill-defined; Violet was assuming the father's part while he was learning the mother's. But time ran out on them, and in the uncertainty and confusion Barney slipped through the net.

ONE night, looking down on the privet jutting from the dark pool of Violet's garden, Albert is put in mind of Pompeii and his mom. In respect to the former, how its excavators uncovered what they believed to be the mast tops of the city's stranded fishing fleet but which deeper digging proved to be a cypress grove; in respect to the latter, how at a recent Friday dinner he had noticed her uncharacteristically staring off into space. Albert asked her what she was looking at. Albert's dad, sitting alongside her on their couch, responded, " 'Gazing upon Broadway's busy scene,' " and they both smiled. Albert said they had him there all right, and that he sure was in the old dark. His dad explained that fifty years ago, when Albert's mom appeared on the Broadway stage, the lead of a Sunday feature on her began, "Gazing upon Broadway's busy scene . . ." Albert asked how come he had never heard this before. "As I believe I told you," his dad said, "there's a lot about us you don't know." Among them, Albert later realizes, is what his mom was looking at.

These speculations, indicating once again the fallibility of presuppositions, lead to the reflection that although figures diminish as the space between them and the observer grows, time can magnify. Thus Barney now looms larger than in life, whirling out of the darkness like the Black Monk, towering unsteadily in the garden, so that his terrified face is at Albert's window—huge, pale, unshaven, mutely appealing—as it was when Barney last kissed him goodbye. When Barney told him over the phone from Wisconsin, a month before he returned to New York and disappeared, forever, from LaGuardia— he was found a month after his twentieth birthday in the Hudson River—that he was running twenty miles a day, that he was going to win the marathon at the Moscow Olympics, why hadn't Albert made the connection and realized that Barney was losing his mind? Was it because there was the possibility, however remote, that he was a prodigy, that he *would* win, that he would make something of his life?

"Did you remember the alimony?" Violet asks Albert. She is lying in the tub, with only her head above the surface. Gazing upon her submerged form, Albert recalls that Augustine had gone to a certain public bath after his mother's death because he had heard that its name was derived from the Greek for driving sadness from the mind, but that "the bitterness of sorrow could not exude out of my heart."

"As my dad would say," Albert says, producing the check from his pocket, "I prepare my trousers the night before."

Once, when Albert asked him to run through this nifty little procedure, his dad had said, "Before retiring, I remove the contents of the pockets—coins, my keys, penknife, and so forth—of the trousers I'm wearing and transfer them to the pockets of the trousers I've set out for the next day—"

" 'What's the big hurry?' I always ask him," Albert's mom said, chiming in. "And do you know what he tells me? 'I am the foe of disorder.' "

"While doing so," his dad went on, "I glance at the memoranda I've jotted down in the course of the day and put in my pockets. Some of these I may transfer from pocket to pocket as many as a half-dozen times until the operative date of the matter I have to remember, when I dispose of them. I recommend you follow my example."

In his mind, Albert sometimes reverses this process of his dad's, so that the foe of disorder, interminably rummaging in his pockets under Albert's mom's skeptical gaze, becomes progressively younger each day, as does she, while he transfers their contents, until Albert's mom vanishes and the young man who is to become his dad, having arrived at his wedding eve, is alone with his little pile of belongings and memoranda, one of which, reading "Wedding, 11 A.M., June 25," he methodically tears into many pieces.

"And how *is* your father?" Violet asks, lifting an arm to take the check. To Albert, this seems a prodigious occurrence—the pale arm unexpectedly rising, dripping, from the depths, like that of the Lady of the Lake.

Prodigies! Is this what the pinnules foretold, these mournful interludes in this vaporous place? After the fern's decline, Albert recalls, everyone else lost interest in it, and the spraying ceremony was no longer observed; it was left to him to lug the diminished plant to the tub and dutifully sprinkle its few remaining fronds. As he usually took care of the fern after his morning shower, while he was still naked, at night he often discovered several pinnules entangled in his pubic hair. These evoked vague longings, as though they were evidence of pagan revels in which he had been permitted to take part, on the condition that all memory of them would be erased.

"Limping," Albert replies at last. "He told me that he and his secretary were walking down the corridor to his office, and that he was imitating her rather emphatic step by stamping his feet on the marble. 'But I was not entirely satisfied with the amount of noise I was making,' he told me. 'I had failed to reproduce her tread.' 'So what did you do?' I asked. 'I leapt in the air,' he said. 'And when you came down?' 'I fell.' 'You got carried away,' I said. 'Even I go to extremes,' he told me."

Albert envisions his eighty-one-year-old dad at the height of his leap, in the long, dim corridor faced with marble the color of old bones, striving to free himself from time's grip; and he also sees Barney, momentarily suspended in the dark over the river—Albert has persuaded himself that it had lain entrancingly, dark and darker, full of speculative gleams, in the path of his headlong flight from reality—seeking surcease from *his* torments. Fifteen years before—thin, white, naked, aloft—Barney soared past the door of Albert and Violet's bedroom on his way to the bathroom. "Don't look!" he cried in midair, but Albert, dazzled, could not avert his eyes. Now—shouldering the blame for Barney's death in the same spirit with which he yearned to circle under less specific griefs—he realizes that this time he had turned aside, and that Barney had passed from view forever.

As though with aching arms, Albert bears upraised the memory of that first frantic leap, just as the massive "Feast of the Rose Garlands" was conveyed through snowy mountain passes, for when Rudolf II, the Holy Roman Emperor, acquired it he deemed it too precious to be transported by a carriage, which might overturn, and had it bundled in rugs and carried upright across the Alps from Venice to his citadel in Prague by relays of strong men.

TEN

~~~~~~~~~~~~~~~~

ALBERT TELLS DR. NEDERLANDER that everything women say to men can be reduced to ten basic expressions, all of which begin with "Why don't you . . ." Dr. Nederlander nods noncommittally. Albert goes on to say he arrived at this when the Human Dynamo said to him, "Why don't you ever take me dancing?"

"Why don't you?" Dr. Nederlander asks.

"That's irrelevant in this context," Albert says. "It struck me that Violet had said the very same thing, as had a number of girls I knew before I married her."

"Aha! *Das Aha-Erlebniss!*" Dr. Nederlander murmurs.

"As you will," Albert says. "Another of the Top Ten is 'Why don't you make love to me anymore?'—which, of course, is why I'm here."

"Of course," Dr. Nederlander says, perhaps, Albert detects, a little doubtfully.

Here is a six-story building with a good address on the East Side, in which Dr. Nederlander has had an office since he gave up his apartment on West End Avenue and moved to New Jersey, where he tramps about his property playing his accordion or systematically cutting down trees with his power saw. Make that *offices*, as Albert discovered when he started going to him again after a lapse of five or six years. His initial shock had been the first-floor waiting room, which resembled the Port Authority Bus Terminal, being dismally crowded with lounging blacks and ethnics. As he further discovered, the upper stories were divided into cubicles identically furnished, down to the Utrillos on the walls, through which he could hear disharmonious and unrewarding lamentations. If, like a doll house, the façade were missing, Albert felt sure that an array of fifty therapists would be revealed, nodding in concert as though obedient to a central baton, their fifty patients straining on their couches as though trying to burst the bonds that tied them to themselves—a struggle in several ways reminiscent of C——'s.

"Hey, what is this," Albert said during his first session, "some kind of plain-pipe-rack 19 Berggasse?"

"I believe we have the odd podiatrist," Dr. Nederlander said.

The cubicles gave off corridors at whose turnings Albert might suddenly be confronted with psychiatric couches standing on end, like rearing horses, so that their ripped cambrics were revealed; in much the same manner, those who had reclined on them over the years had bared their rent psyches, although, Albert acknowledged, it was their particular natures that the former disclosed their undersides while vertical, the latter while horizontal. This insight set off unspecified reverberations, like the buzzings and rattlings behind his back whenever he typed; Albert was never able to determine which objects in his living room produced the noises, because, as he told Dr. Nederlander, when he stopped typing to investigate, they ceased vibrating.

"I may be on the verge of a major epistemological breakthrough," he said.

"Turn your desk around, Albie."

"Dr. Nederlander, that's like asking me to turn my life around, and if I could do that, I wouldn't be here."

Each Thursday evening, when Albert has his appointment, the receptionist directs him to a different office. She presides over a great board equipped with buzzers and lights, by means of which, like an air-traffic controller, she brings the patients safely up and down, making sure that two troubled souls don't violate one another's space in their venturings above. Although Albert is always told where to find Dr. Nederlander, he nonetheless has the impression they are playing a gloomy game of hide and seek, and that there is some sort of therapeutic benefit to be derived from his ability to track Dr. Nederlander down.

"Why can't I make love to her anymore?" Albert asks.

"Why were you able to make love to her for so long?" Dr. Nederlander shoots back.

"Why don't you knock off the sophistry?"

"Everything patients say to their therapists can be reduced. . . ."

MORE is to come. Lying on his back at the bottom of the room at first light—the Human Dynamo had removed the frame of the bed so that the box spring rested on the floor—this is what Albert is thinking. There is so much emptiness between them and the ceiling, which, because the uncurtained windows are set high in the wall, is the brightest part of the room, resembling the surface of the sea seen from below. Indeed, at high tide there are traceries of moving water on the ceiling; the Human Dynamo now lives in Fair Haven, a community of a hundred homes guarded by two decapitated plaster lions and a speed bump, which extends like a gnarled finger into Long Island Sound.

Albert has been going with the Human Dynamo for five years, or since shortly before he separated from Violet, and he has been ineluctably sinking. In the converted pool house in New Canaan, which she was renting furnished when Albert met her, she slept in a high maple bed, presumably Early American. This her landlord, a retired investment banker in his eighties, subsequently removed, replacing it with one several inches lower. (An involved story went with this exchange. The Human Dynamo told it to Albert in bed during a rain delay in the Yankee game they were watching on television, but he hadn't paid attention. He was thinking of the Headless Landlord, as years later he would dwell on the Bodyless Ex-Lovers. Albert occasionally caught glimpses of him at night in the windows of the house across the pool—that is, of him from the waist to the neck. "He's extremely tall," the Human Dynamo had said when Albert first marvelled at the apparition. The bedroom reeked of chlorine; the still black water of the pool promised the concealment of ever greater prodigies. "I think the magic is going out of our relationship," Albert had said.)

When the Human Dynamo rented the second-floor apartment in the two-story house in Fair Haven, she and

Albert perforce lay as entwined as wisteria in a single bed with a wicker headboard belonging to her landlady, which was lower still, until Albert gave her a check to buy a king-size. This turned out to be built even closer to the floor; moreover, the extra width permitted them to lie addorsed on either side, a waste of bedclothes stretching between.

"You know," Albert said upon awakening one morning, "at times I get the impression we're guarding a national monument or something. But commemorating what?"

"The battlefield upon which we lost our lyricism," she murmured.

He was on one elbow, gazing down at her pretty face, whose shape always reminded him of home plate. "That doesn't sound like you," he said.

"That's because almost from the start you discouraged my intelligence."

One evening, when Albert came up from New York to see her, he found that she had taken the bed frame apart and put it away, leaving him stranded.

"What's going on around here?" he asked.

"I'm trying to bring you down to my level," she said.

Reviewing his gradual descent, Albert felt that the beds had been whisked out from under him the way magicians remove tablecloths without disturbing the settings.

Albert turns his head to look out the windows. As always, what he sees are three oblongs of sky. It is early morning and they are as pale as clam shells; the view is without perspective and, Albert feels, is more expressive of disappointment than promise. An egret emerges in the window to his right, by its whiteness revealing the sky to be greyer than Albert thought, fills the frame, its wings stately folding and unfolding, passes from view, reappears in the middle window, vanishes, crosses the window to Albert's left, and disappears. The last he sees of it is its trailing yellow legs, their intricate reticulations. Albert reflects that its progress was such that it might have been pulled from off stage, like the swans in *Swan Lake*. So undeviating has his own passage become, he speculates, that he, too, may as well be at the mercy of some great windlass in the wings.

Albert is unresistingly drawn into sleep. He is awakened by a bird singing "The Colonel Bogie March."

"Did you ever hear a bird whistle the opening bars of 'The Colonel Bogie March'?" he whispers in the ear of the Human Dynamo, who is still sleeping.

"Where?"

"Am I to infer that you *have* heard one, but elsewhere?"

"What?"

"I am trying to determine from your response whether in fact there *is* a bird that whistles 'The Colonel Bogie March,' which you've had occasion to hear, but that Fair Haven is outside its range, or whether—"

"Oh." This a groan.

"Oh, *what*?"

"Oh, you're being Talmudic again."

"It was just a simple Q. & A."

"Albert, you've got to come to grips with the fact that we're separated by a profound socioreligious gap."

"I thought it was a metaphorical battlefield."

"Now *this* is what I call a metaphor," Albert tells the Human Dynamo that night. They had walked to the end of the pier extending from the Fair Haven beach, and down the flight of stairs to the float, upon which they are now sitting. However, since it is low tide, the float isn't floating; it is resting on the mud. "Us," Albert goes on, beginning a vague but comprehensive gesture. How much of the view, or their predicament, he intended to encompass, the Human Dynamo could only infer, because he suddenly arrests his arm, extends it, and points out over the Sound. Where a foot or so of water covers the bottom is a train of little gleams. It advances, shimmering, toward the beach, becoming gradually extinguished at the rear as it is kindled in front, so that it remains the same length. "What is it?" Albert says in awe.

"A duck."

Straining his eyes, he realizes that the scene is not uniformly black, as he assumed, that at the head of the train is a yet blacker object, which resolves itself into a duck, and that the glimmering train is its wake, this or that light from shore being reflected in the rippled surface of the Sound. As the egret defined the day, the duck set forth the night. And how, Albert thinks, is he determined? When he was vacationing in Key Biscayne not long ago, the girl who took care of the motel pool told him one morning that the previous evening she and her husband had tried to reach him to have dinner with them at this little Indian place. She had even called the health-food restaurant where he ate every night, hoping he might be able to join them for jellabees and coffee. "But they don't know my name," Albert said. She was idly vacuuming the pool, the great hose hitched around her waist like Minos' tail. "I asked them," she said, "if there was a grey-haired man eating alone."

Albert visualized the long row of diners at the counter, bent over their spinach soufflés, as if inclined in prayer—

the dim, conceivably ecclesiastical light and the virtuous thoughts to which mung bean sprouts and seaweed give rise strengthened this impression—and for the first time it struck him that at forty-eight he might well be the oldest among them. Did he really stick out? He had never thought of himself as being all *that* grey. For that matter, he never thought of himself; that is, of the figure he cut. Pursuing this line, he concluded that he never considered himself as being older than those who were in fact younger than he, like the Human Dynamo, who was now thirty-two; he only seemed to be aware of the age of older people. How long, he wondered, with a more precipitous sinking feeling than he had experienced *in re* the beds, would that be the case?

Peering into the dark, he recalls that the day he was leaving Key Biscayne to return to New York, the girl gave him a loaf of zucchini bread she had baked. His secretary recently presented him with a half-dozen homemade rugelach, and one of the copy readers at the office had given him a miso cupcake. What was it about him that produced this sudden outpouring of baked goods? Did he seem forlorn or undernourished? A wave of self-pity, like the swell of the incoming tide now gently rocking the float, agitates him.

"How come you never bake any cookies for me?" Albert asks the Human Dynamo.

"I don't give sympathy," she says. "I give advice."

Holding hands, they wend their way back to her house. The curving streets are overarched by trees, intensifying the darkness. Albert feels there is something charmed about the scene—the deep silence, the leafy vault, the winding way. He imagines them as seen from above, through gaps in the foliage. Fondling his scaly tail, Minos

—again!—broods in a dormer window, and stays his hand.

A hurtling cyclist, unseen until the last moment because he (or she) has no light, nearly crashes into them and vanishes, and Albert is put in mind of the first time he encountered the Human Dynamo. Along with one of his fellow editors, he was taking part in the New Canaan Christman Bird Count, poking about some hedges bordering Weed Street, which were supposed to harbor a winter wren. She passed by on her bicycle, furiously pedalling, her ass tilted heartbreakingly to Heaven. (Like a Hassid, Albert mused at the time, watching her diminishing figure through his binoculars, she intimately links Heaven and earth independent of ritual mediation.)

"Not home," the editor said, backing out of the hedges. "What you got there?" He raised his binoculars. "You ought to put that on your life list," he said. The editor knew her slightly; they had bought their BMWs from the same dealer, and had met at the three-thousand-mile check. Albert called her and took her to dinner and a George Segal movie, the first of many of his they went to together.

"Do Jewish people—" the Human Dynamo said on the way to her car.

"We're not Jewish *people*," he said. "We're just Jews."

"Do *Jews* think of George Segal in terms of his Jewishness?"

"What do you mean?"

"I mean, is going to a George Segal movie a Jewish experience?"

"Not like going to the bathroom, if that's what you mean."

When gentiles go to the bathroom, he reflects later

that evening, observing the Human Dynamo leaning tranquilly back against the tank, her purple panties with the yellow competition stripes about her ankles, her arms folded across her chest, they look as though they are riding on a cross-country bus. Jews sit behind closed doors, hunched forward as if condemned to occupy the corners of pediments, chins in their right hands, left forearms across corresponding thighs, enumerating their inveterate sadnesses.

When she joins him in bed, they watch a Yankee game.

"If you'd stop waving it around," she says, "I could see what was happening."

"But nothing's happening."

"Something's *always* happening. Don't project your inertia on the Yankees."

"But they're changing pitchers."

"Marcus Aurelius said, 'All things take place by change.'"

"Marcus Albertus said, 'But not always for the best,'" Albert says, closely observing the *tableau vivant* on the mound. If they weren't wearing baseball uniforms, he thinks, would anyone know what they were up to? If the attitudinizing figures in "The Apotheosis of Henry IV" were dressed as New York Yankees, would Rubens's painting be merely absurd, or would it still resplendently evoke transitoriness and tragedy? If the Human Dynamo and he, naked and outsprawled on the bottom of this darkened room, like drowned men, were on display, would those who viewed them be able to discern that they were drifting apart? Or would there have to be a label on the frame?

Unlike, say, the GNP, Albert reflects as Gossage warms

up, relationships between men and women don't rise and fall; they are at their height at the outset, and inevitably decline. Did he cry out "Stop the car!" on the access road of the Bridgeport airport five years ago in a desperate attempt to preserve that flourishing moment, that *tempus beatum*, to arrest the decay? At any rate, the Human Dynamo stopped her BMW, he flung open his door, she flung open hers, and they ran around to the back of the car, where they embraced. How marvellously true to life it was that they met by the trunk! If Albert were George Segal, she Glenda Jackson or Susan Anspach or Jane Fonda, he would have raced to the back of the car and she to the front; then, skidding, nearly losing their balance, he would have torn around to the front and she to the back. Next Albert to the back, she to the front . . .

ANOTHER night, tide in, water lapping at the sea wall, they walk on top of it in single file, their nostrils full of iodic and melancholy odors; on their right are the lawns of the houses fronting the Sound.

"You're sure we're not trespassing?" Albert says to the Human Dynamo, who is in the lead.

"I always walk here when there's no beach."

At that moment, a terrier materializes on the wall in front of her and starts barking. Spotlights go on, illuminating the lawn, the wall, themselves, the water; next, living-room lights. Through a picture window, Albert sees a woman approaching, peering out.

"Of all the *nerve*," she says in a braying whiskey voice. "Just what do you think we pay our dues to the Association for, I ask you? Of *all* the nerve. Of all *the* nerve."

The lights, the barking dog, the coarse voice sounding as

though it were issuing from a loud-hailer, makes Albert feel as though he has been detected sneaking across a border. He turns and begins to retrace his steps. Looking over his shoulder he sees that the Human Dynamo hasn't moved. She is standing on the wall in her BMW racing team jacket, her hair extraordinarily blond in the stark light.

"*Of* all the nerve." There, she's rung all the changes, Albert notes. As far as he can tell, she is alone; evidently her appeals are to a higher authority—the same party, he supposes, who wields the inexorable baton in Dr. Nederlander's office building. If he hadn't been with the Human Dynamo, there would have been no alarm, he concludes. It was he and his kind that the headless lions were intended to menace, the pedimental fugitives who made her kind wait outside the bathroom door at country inns. If he were George Segal, he'd caper about the lawn, scratching his flanks like a chimpanzee, telling her and her Association where they could put their cute little peninsula—mixing invective with wit, of course, so it would play.

"Just how do you expect us ever to make love again if you keep lying on your back staring at it in wonder?" the Human Dynamo says when they are in bed.

"But you went and turned the Yankee game on."

"We used to make love when the Yankees were playing."

"But they weren't any good then. It didn't matter if they won. They were background music. [La-dah-dah-dah-*dum.*] Now every game is *crucial.*"

Awakening in the middle of the night, Albert hears a tennis game in progress—the faint pops of the ball striking the rackets. Fair Haven's two clay courts are only a block or so away, but he wasn't aware that there were lights for night play. Pop, pop. Pop, pop. Albert neither plays tennis nor skis—another battlefield separating him from the Human Dynamo, whose unrelenting pursuit of these sports and cycling gave rise to her name. Pop, pop. Pop, pop. No one is playing tennis, he realizes. The pops are the exhalations of the Human Dynamo's breath. This discovery strikes him as being almost unbearably poignant: the image that comes to mind is of her being unable to find a partner and so reduced to playing interminable sets of tennis with herself in her sleep. Poignancy will be my ruin, he thinks. As other men are undone by avarice, ambition, grand passions, he will sink—is sinking—under a burden of tender sorrows, which, like snowflakes, singly are nearly weightless, but heaped on a roof can buckle it. An example of reverse *lacrimae rerum*, he reflects, would be his dwindling supply of argyle socks. In this case, the fewer that remain in his sock drawer, the more affecting the emotion.

Tap. Pop. Tap. Pop. Tap, tap. Pop. Taptaptap. Pop.

Now it's raining, Albert says to himself. A hell of a doubles match.

"I heard it," the Human Dynamo says, awakening.

"I know, it's raining."

"Not the rain. Howard."

"Howard? Oh yes, good old Howard. One of those space salesmen you hit with."

"Howard's a parrot."

"I'd never have guessed."

"He lives next door."

"I always said Fair Haven didn't let just anyone in."

"Howard whistles 'The Colonel Bogie March.' "

"Another mystery down the drain," Albert says sadly. "Life never lives up to the expectations that its theme music promises."

"*Our* lives, Albie."

"As you keep saying, we've got nothing in common."

"Well, do we?"

"Yes. Although we're incompatible, we're both incapable of breaking up."

ALBERT's hotel room in Madison is on the third floor, overlooking the lake, which is unexpectedly vast, sealike, the far shore barely discernible. The hotel is built right on the water, so that when he stands back from the picture window, he can't see the shore below; the impression is that the hotel rises out of the lake, its foundation green with algae, at which long, shadowy fish languidly nibble. This romantic illusion is heightened by the lurid colors the evening sky imparts to the water, the wave-tossed surface, and, as it becomes darker, bats perilously veering by the window.

Albert had come to Madison to see Greta, with whom Barney was living before he fled to New York. He had paid for her plane ticket so she could come to the funeral, but he hadn't gotten the chance to speak to her about Barney then; he told her he would fly out to Madison sometime—she was a phys ed major at the university— and they would talk.

Now Albert is sitting on one of the twin beds in the hotel room, speaking on the phone to the Human Dynamo in Fair Haven.

"Then we played a little nine-ball."

"Who won?"

"She did."

"But you weren't really trying. You were attempting to dazzle her by making like George Segal with the massé and jump shots."

"I was trying. I always try to do my best, you know that."

"You don't always try to be nice to the Dynamo."

"That may be because Albie finds it hard to relate to people who take refuge in the third person."

"You're so out of touch with your own feelings, to say nothing of mine, that I sometimes think it's the only way to reach you."

"Barney taught her."

"Taught her what?"

"To shoot pool. He taught me, too. He could run the table. That's his legacy. Greta and I are his disciples. And she's now older than he ever was. I can't rid myself of the feeling that we're leaving him farther and farther behind. It's almost as if he is trapped somewhere and struggling, and that through neglect or a lack of application we're not doing our best to find and free him, as we failed to come to his aid when he was alive."

"What else did she tell you?"

"That he didn't eat or sleep, that he roamed about all night. Days were consumed in sentences, weeks in paragraphs. The more she said, the less I recognized him. He kept changing shape; he dwindled away. Before long she was talking about someone I never knew. It was as if she were telling me her dreams, and I found myself not listening."

"I told you you shouldn't go. But by then it was too late. You tell me everything after it's taken place. Letting Violet take the garden apartment in your building because you felt sorry for her, flying to Madison because you felt sorry for yourself. It's as if I'm reduced to writing letters to the editor. You've put me on the fringes of your life. I can't improve our relationship from there."

Neither of them say anything for a while. At last, she goes on. "Then what did you do and what did she do?"

"We bought frozen yogurts."

"Did you sleep with her?"

"What makes you say something like that?"

"You're always wanting to complete circles."

In the dark, the lake sounds like a running toilet. Albert feels overwhelmed by wetnesses, greennesses, stoninesses; the bats trying to penetrate the picture window, the fishes' slow undermining, Barney streaming with the tide. His coffin was so unexpectedly light, the pallbearers, the huge, loping kids he'd played basketball with, nearly lost their balance when they lifted it to leave the church.

The declivity on the other bed appears to Albert like the settled surface of a grave into which the earth has been newly shovelled.

"If we were spies," Albert says to the Human Dynamo, "we could pass on state secrets and no one could overhear us."

"But we're not," she says. "We're ex-lovers, and no one is listening to us because we no longer have anything new and interesting to say."

They are standing in the surf off the coast of South Carolina, with the water up to their necks, so that their heads appear to be bobbing on the surface like floats come loose from fishermen's nets.

"As far as anyone can tell," Albert says, "we don't have any bodies. I suppose it's because we don't have any more use for them, like our tails."

"You can't see us hanging upside down from a branch, chattering to each other? It does sometimes seem we've been together millions of years."

"What I can see is us in your BMW going to LaGuardia the morning after I made love to you for the first time."

"That was at least a *thousand* years ago. The last time, too, I wouldn't doubt. Same millennium, anyway."

At least, Albert thinks, because she had been wearing a miniskirt, and he had kept his hand on the inside of her revealed thigh all the way down the Merritt. It had been so early in the morning—she was catching the first flight to Detroit—that there wasn't any traffic. She must have driven eighty-five miles an hour the whole way. But, Albert reflects, surface diving, no matter how fast she drove how many times, they would never arrive at the airport in time to prevent Barney from plunging off.

In the underwater murk, he gently takes hold of the Human Dynamo's ankles and yanks her down. Whether her burbled utterance is a laugh or a shriek, he can't tell, but, watching the bubbles issuing from his mouth—each, he fancies, conveying a letter to the surface, like an S O S tapped on the hull of a disabled sub—he knows that his blub-blub-blub is, "Now we no longer exist."

THAT night, Albert awakes in their hotel room to find himself, like a dog scrabbling at the earth after a buried bone—not a specific bone, necessarily, but one of the hoard of numberless bones strewn and intermingled and forgotten that the earth encloses—tearing at his forehead with his fingernails, as if trying to uncover a thought, a system of thought, from the great disorderly pile locked inside.

"What have you gone and done now?" the Human Dynamo says in the morning, seeing the terrible gash, the dried blood on the pillow.

"I was trying to remember."

"Remember what?"

"That's it."

"Albie," she says, reaching out, possibly to smooth his hair, "ex-lovers can love each other, can't they?"

"Maybe that was it."

"Was what?"

"The answer to your question."

If Frege were right, Albert reflects, when he wrote that thoughts cannot be created but only grasped, all that came to hand were the birds twittering on the plane to Charleston. He had been half asleep when he heard the first one. Someone's bringing his caged bird south on his lap, he concluded, and has taken the cloth off. Then he heard another, and still another. Must be a big bird show going on somewhere.

"Plane's full of little twittering birds," he muttered to the Human Dynamo, who was sitting alongside him.

"What ever are you talking about?"

"Listen."

"I am listening."

"Then don't you hear them?"

"Albert, what I hear are those little electronic games."

"I bet George Segal would have something to say at a time like this."

"But it wouldn't be that still more magic is going out of our relationship."

"I KNEW it would happen," Albert tells Dr. Nederlander the next time he sees him.

"I'm not going to guess, Albie."

"You're not going to have to, I'm going to tell you. I

open your office door and I catch you with your hand inside an analysand's blouse. Don't talk, *I'm* the one that's paying. That's right, wrong office, wrong therapist, probably not a therapist at all because they don't mess around, it has to be one of the podiatrists. But what does it *mean?*"

"What does *what* mean?"

"Hey, this is your bag, Doc. Me bursting into the wrong office."

"Albert, everything you do doesn't have to have significance."

"Yes, but *something* has to. Remember how when I used to see you before, we talked about my rut, how you wanted me to rent a car and go antiquing in Connecticut, anything that was *different?*"

"You *ought* to be an antiquarian," Dr. Nederlander says. "You really like circling back."

"To where?"

"To Violet, the Human Dynamo."

"Barney. I keep dreaming about him. Last night he confessed he'd been hiding in Mamaroneck. He said he thought I'd punish him for running away. Oh, do I have a good one for you. This morning I went down to Violet's to walk the dog. I got the collar and the leash and was on my way out when I heard her calling from her bed. 'You forgot something,' she said. 'What did I forget?' I said. 'You forgot the dog,' she said. I had, and I was half out the door. I've got to be on the verge of a major phenomenological breakthrough."

"Which reminds me, what about all the buzzing and rattling?"

"I've got a new carpet. *Alles schläft.* Now *you* tell *me* something, Dr. Nederlander. Is the ceiling of this office higher than the others, or did you bring your power saw to the office and cut down the legs of the couch?"

"I'll give you a lift to the subway," Dr. Nederlander says, rising. "I'm late for this course I'm taking."

"What's that, 'The Psychopathology of Narcissistic Tranquillity'?"

"No, 'Small Gasoline Engines.' "

Crossing Central Park, Albert says, "Every time I go to Violet's to walk the dog, I'm overwhelmed anew."

"You do get easily overwhelmed."

"You would too, if half the furniture down there was yours. How would you like to be on permanent loan exhibition. It's a fucking marriage museum!"

"You told her she could hang on to the furniture because your apartment was furnished."

"I said it, but it was because I felt sorry for her. You think I'm a nice guy, don't you, Dr. Nederlander?"

"I think you deserve the all-around camper award, Albie."

Albert looks out the car window at the perspective of dark solemn domes of foliage, like the swelling prominences of a Middle Eastern city. Serene visions and contemplations of mosque and Moorish give rise to their joint near-homophone, morose; this in turn calls to mind a week he spent with the Human Dynamo at a Western ski resort, mood taking precedence over conflicting angularity. She had made a terrific scene one foggy morning before the lifts opened, crying out that she would have to kill herself in front of him for him to realize how far he had let her down.

"Don't you remember the girl who lived in the pool

house?" she said, waving her roaring blow dryer about, as though it were the weapon with which she was going to do herself—or him—in. "Can't you see what you've done to her?"

"What have I done?" he said, evading a blast of hot air. "You left her alone."

Albert regretfully acknowledged that he had heard this line before, too, from Violet, and the theme and thrust of his life suddenly stood revealed: he was irresistibly drawn to disillusionment—and disillusioning—because it was from the rubble of dashed hopes that he fashioned his slight and sentimental art.

Her tears nearly dried, the Human Dynamo insisted he accompany her to the tram terminal, so he could watch her ascend the mountain. In a din of clattering boots and skis, they shuffled forward in the line that snaked around and around the barriers, as though proceeding to the tellers' windows in some stony, infernal bank. At one point, he was asked to step aside, for he didn't have a ticket. The tram arrived, emerging from the fog. As the attendant flung open the gates and the skiers surged forward, he heard above their jocular mooing someone calling his last name. He turned and saw it was the Human Dynamo. She had never used it before. She was in high gear, hurtling down Weed Street. In the distance, two middle-aged men were peering into the shrubbery, as though in its crepuscular recesses they had at last found, as Dr. Johnson wrote of Pope's grotto, "a place of silence and retreat, from which he endeavoured to persuade his friends and himself that cares and passions could be excluded."

Later, swimming laps in the pool at the lodge, the vapor rising from the superheated water commingling with the descending mist, so that he was all in whiteness, snow-flakes settling coldly on his arms and back, Albert imagined the tram rising, swaying, vanishing. When she got to the top of the mountain, she was going to ski down the other side, a tiny, determined figure against the enormity of the slope—so much like Violet on the expanse of sheets, he recalled when, despairing, she clenched herself into a miserable ball—and never come back.

Turning to Dr. Nederlander, Albert says, "You know, Tolstoy said that playing the accordion diverts men from realizing the falsity of their goals."

"You want me to turn on the Yankee game?" Dr. Nederlander says.

ELEVEN

~~~~~~~~~~~~~~~~~~~~~~~~~~~~~~~~~~~

SUCH IS THE ALLURE of the written word that if we could
see through walls we would be appalled by what met our
gaze: thousands, *tens* of thousands of haunted men and
women in lonely kitchens, second bedrooms, and sun
porches, hunched over typewriters, striving for literary
fame, the faint, intermittent clatter as mournful as rain
spattering on fallen leaves, which, Kafū the Scribbler tells
us, is a stronger agent to move men's hearts than cataracts.

Now and again, Albert has been afforded glimpses of a
number of these undaunted souls—Skippy Mountjoy,
bowed beneath the privet, for one—engaged in what Dr.
Johnson called "the epidemical conspiracy for the destruc-
tion of paper." So have we all. You may apprehend Albert
in the window, third floor front behind the pot of morning-
glories, given to self-dramatization, wondering whether
he is repeating himself, and smoking a cigar.

Years ago, Albert was taken by a mutual friend to meet a man named Parsons who edited the house journal of an oil company. He lived on the outskirts of El Paso with his wife and three children, and had written five novels before breakfast, none of which had been accepted. He said he had high hopes for No. 6, then in progress. His wife, seated beside him on the sofa, ambiguously squeezed his hand. After drinks, Parsons took Albert on a tour of the house; his kids tagged along. Albert towered above them, swaying slightly, like the image of a saint in a religious procession. That, he regretfully gathered, was his role there: He was that venerated figure, the published writer, who might bless or favor Parsons' ineffectual art, his interminable pages. They paused at the door of Parsons' study; it was in the back, commanding a prospect of the desert. Parsons made a diffident gesture, indicating an irregular pile of manuscript that, picturesquely illuminated by the light from the hall, rose from a bridge table like the stump of a ruined marble column. Albert envisioned him at his electric typewriter, the cold blast from the air conditioner ruffling a stack of second sheets, faint with hunger, his inspiration failing, staring at the desert as though hoping that an *Erlebnisträger*, a carrier of experience, would stumble into view and unfold his strange and profitable tale.

Garrulous wayfarers never ring Albert's bell; idly cleaning his typewriter keys with an old toothbrush dipped in rubbing alcohol or laying his cheek against the cold top plate, he tries to recall what has happened to him recently that might move men's hearts. At forty-eight, only one thing that hasn't happened before comes to mind; perhaps this is by design, perhaps a result of a kind of resignation. Not long ago, while talking on the telephone to Violet, he mentioned that he varied his bedtime. "You live so dangerously," she said.

Now and again, Albert wonders what became of Parsons. If life had gone on as before, he would have finished No. 12 or 13 by now. But perhaps he threw in the towel midway through No. 8 and took up, say, jogging instead. Albert visualizes him, pounding through the neighborhood before daybreak, eyes brimming with tears in acknowledgment that the world wasn't at fault for not recognizing his literary merit, but that he had little or none, his wife glancing out the kitchen window in anticipation of his ungainly finishing sprint. Albert pictures, too, Parsons' abandoned typewriter, like Ozymandias' shattered visage, drifted over with the sand that somehow sifts through shut windows in places such as El Paso.

But give him his due; whatever else they lacked, presumably his pages were—are?—coherent. Would Albert could say the same about those so unremittingly typed by his old college roommate Emory Bates on his three ancient office machines in Coconut Grove. These monumental contraptions are arrayed on a long table as though on display in an exhibit commemorating the Industrial Revolution. Emory has a wheeled typing chair, and, Albert gathers, if the muse deserts him at one typewriter, he propels himself in front of another. At such urgent moments, he must appear like a figure in one of Rubens' more tumultuous compositions—his full, fair beard and long hair flying, his glasses pushed to the top of his head like an uplifted visor.

Emory has been keeping what he calls a journal for five years—ever since he became aware that he was vanishing. "Why don't I have an effect on people anymore?" he asked

Albert at the time. "I'm becoming invisible." He sold his health-food store and began typing. Each day got at least a single-spaced page, often two, so that by now he has written more than two thousand pages. These cannot be read; this is not to say they are unreadable, which is pejorative. It is just that the writing is so condensed, so private, so allusive that they are all but unintelligible. They might as well be in cipher. (Suppose you were the first to crack Pepys's or Schlegel's code and found it concealed a laundry list.) Nonetheless, Emory has convinced himself that it is inconceivable that there is nothing of value in two thousand pages. Specifically, it is inconceivable that there isn't a book that can be made into a movie. When on the subject, he skips over whatever this entails so he can get to the part where he steps from the limousine for the premiere. "I've been thinking of wearing a Glenurquhart suit with gray, bronze, and red decorations," he once told Albert, "a blue-jean blue chambray shirt, and a burnt-orange silk tie."

Two thousand pages! Emory yanks at the handle of a filing cabinet drawer, which, because of the great weight of what is within, rolls irresistibly, even majestically, open to its full length, and steps aside so that Albert can view the contents. Instead of two thousand pages, his naked body could be lying there—pale, puffy, careworn—for the journal is not only his life's work, it is also his life. "I find I can't recall anything earlier than nineteen seventy-three," he told Albert on his last visit. "It is as though the past does not extend back beyond the first page of my journal."

It was on this occasion that Emory informed Albert he had appointed him his literary executor. They were in the sleeping porch where he batted out the journal. The room was full of greenish light; Emory lives in an old frame cottage hemmed in by a multifariousness of leaves. In that light, the function of the typewriters, which now protruded from the table like coral heads, seemed mysterious, inexplicable; they could have been obsolete and dilapidated contrivances for making buttonholes. Emory, too, his eyes enlarged behind his glasses, conferring heroic proportions to his entire frame as well as suggesting the marine, in the respect that refraction makes fish, bare feet appear larger underwater, was ruined, mythic, tinged with green—in Albert's fancy algae on marble or, more simply, *verde antico*—as though, with his streaming beard and locks, he was not so much Poseidon, tilted in rage on the seabed, as his statue, which, having tumbled through vertiginous fathoms, was implanted at a fearful angle, eyes, mouth eternally open, stupendously imploring, unable to drown.

"You'll know what to do with it," he went on. "I don't want it falling into the wrong hands. In addition, I would like you to deliver the eulogy at my funeral." Emory had also convinced himself that he would die young, unappreciated, before he had the chance to emerge from the limo. "I want you to tell them I was intelligent."

He rested a hand on one of the typewriters, as one would lay a hand on the head of a faithful setter or a bust of Aristotle. "Maybe the shirt should be orange and the tie blue," he said. "What do you think?"

When Buddy Bloom went to the premieres of his movies he wore a safari jacket and Adidas, no socks. But producing movies didn't gratify him; it is Buddy's conviction that you can't be a success in life unless you write a book. Buddy stopped making movies and wrote an autobiographical novel, *Foreign Bodies*, in his beach house in Malibu. He sent Albert a Xerox of the ms for his comments. Albert wrote back, telling him it wasn't half bad—it wasn't—but that the protagonist was like somebody played by George Segal, and that Buddy Bloom's life was more interesting than George Segal's.

The next time Albert was on the Coast, he had dinner with Buddy. After Buddy took a sip of his white-wine spritzer, Albert asked him what was happening with the book. Buddy told him someone had put him on to this old lady, a German who did freelance editing, and the upshot was she moved in with him so they could whip *Foreign Bodies* into shape.

"I was the first on my block to have a live-in editor," Buddy said. "She could parse the shit out of a sentence, but she wouldn't let up. I'd say, 'What say we knock off so I can clear the head by shooting a *bissel* bumper pool?' and I'd take off for the game room. She'd be right behind me in her fuzzy yellow slippers, popping Tic Tacs and carrying on about my transitions. 'Mr. Bloom,' she'd say, 'your rhythms are too predictable, like a bad dance band from the thirties. A ricky-tick, a ricky-tick, a ricky-tick. Ve *must* wary dem. Ve *vill* wary dem.' 'Before ve undertake dat, Frau Gelberman,' I told her, '*I'm* going to valk on the beach and *you're* going to stay in the house and comb out your schlippers.' 'Mr. Bloom,' she told me, 'the vorld vould not haff *Wallenstein* if Schiller had goofed off by valking on de bich.' 'Frau Gelberman,' I told her, 'there is no bich in Weimar.' 'Mr. Bloom,' she told me, 'you are haffing schport mit me.'

"I was haffing it up to here with her was what I was haffing. I had to get rid of her. But she wouldn't go. So I went. Late one night, after she had gone to bed with a cup of Ovaltine and a couple of chapters, I packed a bag, tippy-toed out of the house, put the Lamborghini into neutral, and pushed it down the Colony until I was out of earshot. Then I drove into the desert and watched game shows in motels. Two days later, I called up. 'Gelberman.' I hung up. I called again the next day. 'I know it's you, Mr. Bloom,' she said this time. 'You can run away from me, but you can't escape your obligations to posterity.' She underestimated me. I drove to the airport, took a plane to New York, and stayed at the St. Regis for a week. Flying back, I had the awful feeling I might find Frau Gelberman's skeleton on my deck, manuscript pages interspersed with bones, but the house was empty."

A year later, as Albert was about to step off a curb at Columbus Circle, he stayed his foot. Stencilled on the pavement was the following: FOREIGN BODIES. A BLOCKBUSTER OF A NOVEL BY BUDDY BLOOM. Buddy always had a flair.

Albert's foot hovered over *Foreign Bodies* in May; now it is October, and nighthawks are swooping about the floodlit tower of the Kismet Hotel and Country Club like lost souls. (I fear Frau Gelberman would decry this transition as an unseemly metastasis.) Albert is in Las Vegas waiting for Bruce Bleibtraub to arrive from Rancho Mirage, so they can go over *Preferential Treatment*, his novel in progress. Like all the enterprises Bruce has involved Albert in over the years, this one started with a phone call in the course of which he said, "I'd like you to do me a special favor." In the past, these favors ranged from Albert using his connections to get him a ringside seat for the second Ali–Frazier fight to picking up a birthday cake Bruce ordered for his daughter, who lived with her mother in Westport, where they didn't know *bupkis* about baking cakes, and sticking it in Albert's refrigerator so Bruce could come by for it after his show because the bakery was closed when he got off the air and he was going up to Connecticut first thing in the a.m.

Until he decided that only writing could fulfill him and went to Rancho to work on his novel, Bruce had a talk show on an FM station and did voice-overs for TV commercials. When the camera girl in the Kingdom of the Deep, the Kismet's gourmet seafood restaurant, where Albert and Bruce ate on Bruce's last night in town, asked him what he did for a living, he said, "I'm an air personality" and grinned prodigally. To his mind, it was all preposterous: his livelihood; the net festooned with corks, Japanese glass floats, and blowfish strung over their heads in whose dusty meshes Albert feared they would become entangled and hauled off for a moral accounting; the camera girl's half-revealed breasts, quivering like quennels of pike—everything but his writing.

When Bruce called he was prepared to fly to New York with the ms: Albert had the wild notion he was going to buy two tickets and get adjoining seats, one for *Preferential Treatment*, the way athletes have been known to travel with massive trophies, musicians with valued instruments. He was elated when Albert told him he was going to be in Vegas, and they could get together there. He insisted that Albert read the ms beforehand—a problem, as he wouldn't entrust it to the mails. Bruce has little faith in public services and leaves nothing to chance. For example, he went to great lengths to seek out the meteorologist who forecast for Rancho, cultivated his friendship, took him and his wife out to dinner, because the public forecast was insufficiently detailed for his purposes.

"A solution has presented itself," Bruce told Albert when

he called the next day. "The parent company that owns the station I worked for is having a convention in Los Angeles, and one of my former colleagues who is attending is more than willing to hand-carry the ms to your office when he gets to New York. I'm driving up this evening to effect the transfer." Knowing Bruce, Albert was sure this arrangement had been set up by a phone call asking for a special favor; and, knowing Bruce, Albert visualized the transfer being effected on a deserted street corner in Beverly Hills, say Rodeo and Elevado.

Albert wasn't clear what function he was supposed to perform *in re Preferential Treatment*—anything, he supposed, from correcting Bruce's spelling to hailing him as a genius.

"Ees not half bad," is what Albert tells him by the Kismet pool, where they are reclining on adjoining chaises, brushing away flies; the air is scented with mown grass and piña coladas. Whenever Bruce solicited Albert's opinion, he addressed him in the guise of a Puerto Rican super or a Chinese laundryman, and expected him to reply in kind; Albert gathers this charade softened anything less than unqualified praise. "But the hero is like somebody played by George Segal," Albert goes on, "and Bruce Bleibtraub's life is more interesting than George Segal's."

This isn't a stock reply; that's the way both mss strike Albert; it must be in the air. Whether Bruce's life is more interesting than Buddy's is a subject to which Albert doesn't address himself; suffice it to say both are more interesting than his. For instance, Bruce often regales Albert with tales of making love with one of his pretaped shows booming out of the Marantzes for background music, of threesomes he videotaped, of his affairs with famous movie stars who, in long, murmurous phone calls in the middle of the night, tell him all the outtasight things their Abyssinian cats have done lately, like mistaking the bowl of grass for kitty litter.

"I know there's a motion picture in it," Bruce says, "but does eet have literary merit?"

"Eet, uh, ees—how you say eet?—eet has, uh, affecting moments." In fact, affecting moments, effectively transferred.

On the way out of the Kingdom of the Deep, Bruce says, "I'd like you to do me a special favor."

Characters in books Albert has read frequently expostulated—those in Buddy's and Bruce's are no exception—but until now never in Albert's life has he uttered what he considered at the time to be an expostulation. "But Bruce—" he expostulates.

"What I'd like you to do is drive me to an adult book store," Bruce says.

As they head down the Strip in Albert's rent car, Albert wonders whether their outing has any connection with his failure to extol *Preferential Treatment*.

"You turn right on East Charleston and go one point one miles," Bruce says.

"How do you know all this?"

"I asked the cab driver on the way in from the airport."

After they have gone point seven miles, Bruce says, "I think we better stop and ask someone."

"Bruce, we haven't gone far enough."

"He could've been wrong. There's a gas station, why don't you stop and ask?"

"If we go a mile and a half, and we haven't come across it, we'll ask."

"Help," Bruce says, "I'm a prisoner in a Chinese meta-phor factory! What we have here is you all over—going on too long, hanging in there when it's dead and buried to make obscure, self-serving points. Your marriage was play-ing to an empty house its last two years. I tell you, we passed it already. It's dark out. Any minute, we'll be in the fucking desert already."

"We've only gone nine-tenths of a mile, Bruce. He said one point one."

"He said it, but he was a shmuck. He had those shmucky allergic-to-smoke signs all over the cab. Stop the car. We need directions. We got to ask somebody who isn't an obvious shmuck. Please, I beg of you, stop!"

Albert pulls over to the curb. Traffic streams silently beyond the closed windows. The arctic blast from the air conditioner blows between them, separating them like a wall of ice. Like Buddy and me, Albert thinks, we don't have much in common, anyway; I'm fascinated by their energy, I suppose they're intrigued by me because I have certain abilities that cannot be energetically attained, and, in a sense, to them I am an *Erlebnisträger* from a more languid world who, once rid of the meshes, would cite, in defense of the charge that he was repeating himself, the morning-glory, which resplendently reiterates itself with-out approbation.

"Metaphors," Albert says, "we got metaphors up the ass! No way you can function by yourself, Bruce. You need a cast of thousands to stage your life, and everything has to be set up in advance, arranged, assured. You've got to know where you are at all times. Me, I do things on my own hook, catch-as-catch-can, stumbling upon dirty books, what my mom trustingly calls human relationships, whatever. Given, a lot of times I come up empty, but there's something to be said for finely distributed sadness, the way darkness imbues the summer sky in a flat place, say Hackensack. It may not lead to an interesting life, but I think it's conducive to a life lived to be put down on paper. That's what's wrong with your hero, Bruce. He's predictable."

"Ah, so," Bruce says, peering intently out the car window, as though straining to will the adult book store into being. "Velly intelesting. But case is, helo of *Plefelential Tleatment* modelled after you."

As though peering through walls, Albert wills into being the manuscript on the bridge table in El Paso, which, successively tinged with violet, with rose, with peach, has grown to a nearly sublime, a precarious height, like those rocky, toppling eminences upon whose summits artists of the late eighteenth century carefully placed tropic birds. He summons up, too, his friend Emory Bates propelling himself, a legless man on a dolly, from one typewriter to another; Buddy pushing the burnished Lamborghini along the Colony, ears pricked for the nemesic flop-flop of Frau Gelberman in the night (But at my back I always hear/Time's fuzzy slippers hurrying near).

Albert wishes it were possible to put his hands gently on theirs, as so many years ago his piano teacher put hers on his, press their fingertips to the typewriter keys, and whisper, "This is the way it is done, this is the way it is done." The impulse brings to mind his forging the endorsement on Barney's income-tax-refund check, which arrived after he was found in the Hudson not far from where, years before, Roger Russek told Albert that integrity had gone out of the world; evidently snagged, his body had been immersed a month. Albert copied the signature from a college application blank Barney had never completed. As he duplicated the signature, Albert discovered how painstakingly, almost devoutly, Barney had written it. Here he had ascended, there he had swooped down; now, like an aviator doing aerobatics, he had inscribed the glorious loop of the "y." As he reproduced the signature, Albert felt Barney's hand on his, guiding the pen, as if telling him, "This was me, this was who I was." If Barney had lived, his signature would have become more ragged—he would have learned to dash it off. So, in a sense, he, too, was an author *manqué*, if only of his name.

DANCING has much the same appeal as the written word. Who doesn't yearn to dance like Fred Astaire? A friend of mine once rapturously described to me Astaire descending the great staircase in the Racquet Club, his little, swift, deft, jaunty, lilting steps. He said Astaire flowed down the marble steps like water. His recitation took a good five minutes and toward the end tears stood in his eyes. (Upon reading this, my friend tells me I am mistaken. Astaire wasn't going downstairs, he was going up. So much apter, that. I rerun it in the cinema of my mind: water gloriously ascending.)

Years ago, on Ponce de Leon, in the Gables, on one of those interminable summer evenings of MISERY and SORROW, Albert noticed a pretty girl of eighteen or so waiting for a bus. The air was still and uniformly lavender, she was wearing white shorts and a pale-yellow T-shirt and she was languorously dancing by herself, beguiling life's monotony away. As far as Albert could see, the city was otherwise deserted; no one was on the sidewalk, there was no traffic; the impression was the bus would never come and that if he parked at a distance and watched, all that would happen would be that finally, astonished, he would realize it had become dark.

Albert only saw the girl twice, once in passing, once as a tiny, solitary, vaguely swaying figure in the rearview mirror, but she beckons to him still, inviting him to join in her wanton dance, mocking his inability to accept, to lift his feet off the ground. "I write the World," Byron said. "I sketch your world exactly as it goes." But, Albert acknowledges, Byron also took part, he briefly leapt in the air, the world he devoted himself to roughing out revolved beneath him, he came down in a different place.

Another example. While he was at the Kismet, waiting for Bruce Bleibtraub, Albert often had occasion to pass the hotel fur shop. This seemed to be open at all hours. Albert gathered this was to accommodate impulse buyers; who knows, a highroller off the New York junket might cash in at 3 A.M. and have an urge to buy a lady friend a palomino fox jacket or a three-quarter wolverine. But only once did Albert see a customer in the store. Usually when he looked in, a woman in her mid-fifties, evidently the proprietress or manager, would be sitting at a reproduction Louis table reading a newspaper. At times she was joined by a man of the same age in doubleknits and a styled hairpiece glittering with spray. The proprietor? The one time Albert saw them with a customer, the man tore coat after coat from their hangers and flung them on the carpeted floor to disclose, as the bucket of water dashed on the unpolished marble slab revealed its variegations, the striping, the definition, the uniformity of flow, the lushness of the skins.

More than once Albert saw these two unattractive people elaborately embracing among the baum marten, fitch and mink, as though demonstrating to window-shoppers that their love was unaffected by the lack of custom. On one occasion, while in each other's arms, they executed a few accomplished dance steps. A waltz it was, slow and sweeping. Their eyelids drooped, their lips parted. As they whirled among the racks of furs, they drew further and further apart, until they were barely touching, being joined only by the lightest application of fingertips, so it appeared that they were about to fly apart. But, Albert recognized, like the time he tied Violet's tie, at that moment they never were more tightly bound.

And once, in an Irish bar, Albert saw two old biddies get up and dance to the jukebox. Sweeter, more piercing than a pine warbler singing on a hot, clear summer day, that— my standard of comparison.

Why are those four men dancing on the mountain pass? What a scene it is! All is white and terrible. Wind is shrieking in their ears, driving snow into their eyes like so many nails, plugging their nostrils, battering them about the body, buckling their knees. So why persist in dancing? I will tell you. Look more closely and you will see they are carrying something. It rises from their midst like a great, taut, white sail, which, catching the full brunt of the wind, slams them this way and that as they stumble toward waiting arms, toward Prague. So, too, we twist and turn, trying to keep a tight grip on what we value, but no one waits down the road to assume our burden.

Guitar and flute play a *gigue* in A minor, andante *con moto*. The melody is taken up by the celli restating the guitar accompaniment pizzicatti, as the oboe replaces the flute motif, *con tristezza*.

About the Author

GILBERT ROGIN was born in New York City in 1929. His short stories have appeared in *The New Yorker, Esquire, Vogue, Mademoiselle, The Reporter, Cosmopolitan* and *Harper's*. His previous books are *The Fencing Master* (1965) and *What Happens Next?* (1971). He is the managing editor of *Sports Illustrated*.